I0822362

Three dreadful childhood tales

HUSH LITTLE BABY

CAYTLYN BROOKE

Hush Little Baby

First published by Kindle Direct Publishing 2023.

First Edition

ISBN hardback: 979-8-9877402-4-8
ISBN ebook: 979-8-9877402-5-5
Visit Caytlyn Brooke's website:
http://caytlynbrooke.wixsite.com/booksbycaytlyn

Editor: Chelsea Cambeis
Proofreader: Samantha Moran
Cover Designer: Neil J Hart

OTHER WORKS

Dark Flowers
Wired
Among the Hunted
The Baker's Wife
Crimson Crisp

For everyone who was never satisfied
with "happily ever after"

TABLE OF CONTENTS

AUTHOR'S NOTE

Dear Reader,

Thank you for picking up this nostalgic, yet dreadful collection. Within these pages you will encounter familiar characters from classic fairy tales and nursey rhymes. Yet, that is where comfort ends, I'm afraid. Contained in each short story, is a healthy splattering of violence, blood, bodily mutilation, and gory descriptions. All these characters are children and have not been aged-up to make this read more pleasant. In fact, it is meant to be quite disturbing. If this collection does not sound like your cup of tea, I urge you to put it down and choose a happier book, perhaps one with a fuzzy duckling on the cover. For those who believe they are ready, remember that children— while devilish and clever—are usually, always two steps behind…

Regards,
Caytlyn Brooke

Goldilocks and the Three Bears was originally titled, *The Story of the Three Bears.* After orally sharing the tale for many years, Eleanor Mure recorded the first written version in 1831 in an illustrated storybook she handmade for her nephew, Horace.

In her tale, the story does not take place in a cottage, but at Cecil Lodge, which was the Mure family estate in Hertfordshire, England. The three bears are friends who wish to live amongst men, and rather than a little girl, an old woman stumbles into their shared home.

However, there is no happily ever after for the trespassing woman. Instead, the three bears try to burn and drown her, but when she remains alive, they throw her atop St. Paul's church steeple, and celebrate their victory.

Similar to the Grimm Brothers' darker collection of stories, Mure's original fairy tale is not the sugary-sweet version we grew up hearing. I too have written a Goldilocks retelling that pushes the envelope even further than Mrs. Mure could have imagined and is certainly not one to whisper to children before bed.

With many nods to the multiple interpretations of Goldilocks and the Three Bears that followed Mure's publication, especially those versions by Robert Southey and Joseph Cundall, hopefully, my rendition will be just right for you.

Enjoy.

Arts & Culture. (2021, January 25). *The Three Bears Before Goldilocks: The History of a Fairy Tale*. Toronto Public Library. http://torontopubliclibrary.typepad.com/arts_culture/2021/01/the-three-bears-before-goldilocks

A GOLDEN AFTERNOON

PART 1

"Golden!" Red shrieked, her pitch rattling the glasses lining the butcher-block shelf. "Give it back!"

Brown crumbs of dry bran tumbled off the other girl's bottom lip as she munched the small slice of muffin she'd pilfered. Golden's jaw warbled as she swallowed greedily. She turned, gave her sister a toothy grin, and pushed the liquified food through the large gap between her crooked front teeth.

"Snooze you lose."

"I was taking a drink."

"It wouldn't have filled you anyway."

Red sank back against the spindled chair, her watery eyes on the second-hand table's chipped jade paint.

"That doesn't mean you can eat her breakfast, Golden." Their mother wrung her hands in the threadbare apron clutching her narrow waist. Her hip bones stood out severely beneath the thin fabric. She was a decimated husk of the powerful woman she used to be. Before the nightmares had descended like that maniacal spider and plagued her every thought. "We don't have much, Golden. I'm already giving you girls my portion. We're a family. We need to share what little we have until I find another job."

Golden rolled her eyes and slunk out of her slouched position.

"Whatever, it's not my fault we're poor." She spat the last word. A sliver of guilt formed, heavy and leaden. The stolen pastry soured in her gut, but she'd meant for her comment to sting. Since their father had fallen victim to his own silver tongue, her emerging insolence had ricocheted into unchecked chaos.

While her mother and sister grieved, Golden's attitude had blackened until her core was soft with brown rot. She brushed the inkling of guilt away with the other gathered crumbs from her too-small cerulean dress and headed upstairs to her and Red's shared room.

"She didn't mean nothing by that, Mama," Red said. Her chair shrieked in protest atop the stained linoleum as she moved to comfort their mother, skinny arms offering what little apology they could.

Golden's bare foot hit the first step. Her mother's reply— if there was one— was lost to the old home groaning under her ascent.

Red entered the loft an hour later. She stepped across the threshold and threw a sweater at Golden's face. "Are you trying to send Mama into another spiral? Why do you have to be so horrid?"

Golden swatted the itchy fabric away. "You started it. I can't wait to get out of here."

Red's lip curled. "Now there's an idea."

Golden narrowed her amber eyes and twirled a long curl around her index finger. "Like you and wolf boy? No, thanks. I don't plan on having any mangy pups anytime soon."

"The amount of enjoyment your cruelty seems to yield astounds me. Tell me, would you crumble into a pile of molten flesh if you were to utter a single kind word?"

Golden sucked her teeth, the sound sharp and wet. Kicking her feet, she pushed herself off the lumpy pillow to rest her soles on the wooden boards. Spreading her legs, she rested her meaty forearms on her thighs as she leaned forward. Her ennui expression hardened. "I'm not the nasty one. If you're looking for a scapegoat, open your eyes. Life isn't a fairytale. Life is dirty and messy and unforgiving. The sooner you and Mama realize there's no handsome prince or golden egg coming to save us from our pathetic existence, the better."

Red sunk to her knees in front of Golden. "But that's exactly why we need to be kind and believe in a magical tomorrow. Without hope of something better, there is nothing to motivate us to work hard to deserve it."

Golden scoffed. "Work hard like Pa, you mean? The only labor he performed was over a bent-over barmaid. Between satiating his carnal desires and drowning in a pint of ale every night, he wasn't left with much opportunity to earn any coin for his family. Add in his weakness for the tables and it's a miracle the collectors only slit *his* throat after they grew wise to his lies, or we'd be buried in that ditch with him."

Red stood, tucking her cropped raven-black hair behind an ear. "I don't want to talk about Pa."

"No, of course you don't. You and Mama clam up every time someone mentions his name. Do you really think he loved us? That he was really going to stop after Mama caught him? You're delusional, Red."

Red pivoted on her heels to face Golden and wrapped her arms around herself, looking small. "He loved me. I know he did. He just lost his way. If Rumpelstiltskin hadn't taken Mary, then—"

"Blame Rumple all you want, but he didn't make Pa do anything. Pa had a darkness in him already. The trickster just exhumed it and gave it legs."

Red fell silent for a long minute and chewed the inside of her bottom lip. "It's going to be different for me. I'm going to make myself a grand life."

"If Wes doesn't breed you by the next full moon."

Striking out with impressive force, Red's palm cracked across Golden's left cheekbone, whipping her head to the side. "Quit talking about things you don't understand. Wes is mine now. Just because he left you once he was sick of your lip doesn't give you the right to insult him. He is a good man who loves me. Stop referring to him as an animal."

Red's chest heaved up and down, her eyes shiny and bright with fury. Golden wiped the narrow trickle of crimson blood from the corner of her mouth with deliberate slowness and smeared her sister's namesake over her porcelain skin. She rose and stepped in front of Red until they were nose to nose.

"He may love you now, baby sister. But just remember the next time he's kissing you that it used to be my name on his lips. My mouth that made him groan. I wonder if you've tried everything we did. Think you'd measure up to me?"

"Get away from me," Red hissed, bristling like an angry cat. "I pray to God the devil takes you. Then maybe you'll understand the hell I've lived these miserable sixteen years as your sister."

Golden's face still stung from the slap. The skin was no doubt a brilliant scarlet and Red's thin fingers were probably imprinted around her eye. "Pray loud then, dear sister. For I'd hate to extend your suffering even one night longer." Her cornflower-blue eyes glistened with malice as the tension crackled between the two. With a smirk, Golden kissed Red's cheek, leaving behind a wet trail of saliva. "I'm going for a walk."

Red shivered and wiped the offensive fluid away with her sleeve. "Where are you going?"

"With luck, to hell."

With a swift slap of her hip, Golden bumped the rickety back door open and grimaced as a wave of heat and sunlight greeted her with the subtlety of a brick wall. The tight bite of her constricting sleeves stoked her temper even more. She had half a mind to tear the infernal material off, but uncomfortable as it may have been, it was her last good dress— at least until she could woo the tailor into gifting her new fabric to replace it.

Golden stalked on and heaved her heavy hair off her sweating neck. In ten minutes, she'd be at the small spring that fed their creek, and she could lounge naked in the sunshine for the rest of the afternoon. Images of Wes cradling her in the cool water formed in her mind, his strong arms supporting her backside while their tongues twisted and tangled together. Out of respect for her sister, she should shun the memory, but Wes had been hers once and the mention of his lips back in their room made her yearn to be held by him again.

Golden ducked beneath a blanket of leaves and slipped into the forest. The pressure in her chest lightened as nature enveloped her, isolating her from the pretentious town and all the people who looked down on her. They whispered of her hardness, her cruelty. They had no idea those characteristics were of her own making. She'd seen what happened to soft-spoken women in their town. Men took everything from them. They reduced the maidens they had once stayed up late writing poetry for to swollen mills in which to produce their sons.

Golden wanted more out of life. That's why she took and demanded; nothing could be achieved by a woman, otherwise. Of course her behavior created enemies and had even driven Wes into her kindhearted sister's arms. But her unyielding reputation was not a source of shame or regret. Rather, it was her armor. She'd sooner be alone and free than ensnared into servitude under the guise of love.

Knocking aside unruly fronds and springy branches, Golden trekked through the woods. Sweat gathered between and beneath her breasts, soaking her chemise. Where was the pond? The creek was on her left, offering a sturdy babble to accompany her thoughts. Surely, she wasn't so distracted that she had missed it.

Golden spun about in a circle, hoping to catch a glimpse of the large flat boulder where she usually lay to dry her hair or a sparkle of sunlight reflecting off the clear water's surface. Yet nothing bespoke that such a place even existed. She fixed her attention on the languid current meandering downstream and considered relinquishing the idea of a refreshing dip and returning home when an appetizing aroma assaulted her senses.

The mouthwatering scent of warm cinnamon and toasted apple danced on the wind. Her stomach growled, already hollow after her pathetic excuse of a breakfast. Even Red's extra portion had done little to placate her hunger. The barren cupboards at home mocked her daily, and the only lunch she had to look forward to was stale bread and lukewarm milk *if* she procured it from the goat herself. Golden took a step toward the west, drawn to the delicious smell like a pulsing beacon.

She spied smoke twisting into the summer sky between the swaying tops of the great oak trees. Edging farther from the creek, Golden inhaled once more, salivating over whatever treat was responsible for the tantalizing scent. What would be the harm in investigating?

As far as she knew, their cottage was the farthest from town. Perhaps a traveler had stopped to prepare a meal over a campfire, unaware he was on the cusp of the village, though Golden wouldn't have recommended the greasy sludge they served at the inn, anyway. Her stride lengthened. Hospitality practically demanded she make herself known and lead the traveler to town— after he offered to share his meal, of course, to show his gratitude.

With her decision made, Golden jogged forward, keeping her target of the wispy smoke in direct sight. The shadowy path brightened as the trees thinned. She slowed her pace, not wanting to appear winded and desperate as she crashed into the clearing. Steadying her weight on a nearby tree trunk, Golden took a few deep breaths and wiped the sweat off her brow. Then again, if she appeared wild and heat ravaged, maybe the traveler would feed her sooner.

Shifting the pine needles from her obscured view, Golden's eyebrows arched as she entered the clearing. Rather than the small campfire she'd pictured, a tall two-story house greeted her. She furrowed her brow. Had she gotten turned around? She glanced up and saw the same curling smoke, and the same delectable aroma flavored the air.

"Strange. I didn't know we had neighbors." Golden proceeded cautiously. Logic dictated that a house meant shelter and safety, but for some reason, her gut clenched with fear the closer she drew. Her steps faltered. Why didn't she know this home?

Golden racked her memory for anything her mother may have mentioned or recollections of hammers or saws that had crescendoed recently through the blue skies. Though with a closer look at the cottage, it appeared old, as if it hadn't been constructed but grown, stretching out of the ground amongst the giant trees. A carpet of spongy green moss layered the roof, hanging off the eaves in long tendrils. The wooden planks were wrinkled, aged skin left too long beneath the sun's stare. Crumbling windowsills drooped above gnarled weeds that choked the few wildflowers that dared show their velvety faces.

Golden wanted to run, to get as far away from that place as possible, but the moment her instincts flared, the scent of honeyed cinnamon grew even stronger— and even more impossible to resist. Sauntering up the dilapidated path, she sidestepped askew bricks and gaping pockets eager to sprain an ankle. Unease squeezed again, fighting for dominance over curiosity and greed.

The front door was cut in half, the lower apron closed, while the top swung open like a missing tooth. Blackness poured forth, and the room beyond was too cloaked by it to make out any details or occupants. The scent was overpowering now, drawing her in like a physical set of arms yanking her closer.

Golden's fingertips hovered over the edge of the closed door, as if the surface might bite. "Hello?" She craned her neck, golden hair dripping into the inky black.

The aroma called from the right and swallowed her last lingering doubts. The half door swung open soundlessly under her touch. As Golden slid her feet across the wood floor, a glint of silver caught her eye. Glancing behind her, she saw identical dead bolts on the sides of both halves. Her gaze slid to the windows. Polished silver locks adorned thick double-paned glass. She frowned. They were brand-new. The smell spiked and recaptured her attention.

Moving farther into the house, Golden noticed it was mostly bare. Picture frames hung in an uneven pattern, but it was too dark to identify the hulking figures depicted within the still shots.

"Hello?"

The front room curved and opened into a cozy kitchen with clean countertops. A butcher-block cutting board lay flat, a large carving knife balanced on the smooth wood, teeth up. A metal canister held an assortment of stirring spoons and a whisk beside it, alongside a large tea mug. Golden wrapped both hands around the base. The ceramic was still warm, and flecks of loose tea leaves clung to the bottom. Fear formed a small pit in her stomach. The home was occupied, and either the homeowner exited from a back door the moment she'd entered the front or they were hiding in the shadows, watching.

Golden set the massive mug back down and turned, anxious to get back to the front door. The house was too quiet, too still. Something wasn't right. Upon pivoting, her eyes fell on a large table in the corner of the room. Three bowls heaped with cream-colored porridge sat on the polished chestnut, and large spoons smiled enticingly. Her stomach groaned again.

"Hello? Is anyone here?" Golden's voice echoed through the empty halls. "Hello?"

The silence was oppressive, almost as if the house were holding its breath. Golden rocked on her heels and bit her bottom lip, eyeing the food. Each bowl was piled high. If she skimmed several bites off the top of each, no one would be the wiser, and she'd gain some much-needed calories.

Golden looked around once more to ensure she was alone. Satisfied, she slunk over to the table and chose the bowl on her left. Gripping the spoon's handle, she dipped the basin into the steaming porridge and brought it to her lips. She only intended to take a bite, but it smelled so good, and she abandoned all manners and loaded her spoon. The flavor of cinnamon she'd caught outside exploded on her tastebuds, along with heat. She should have realized from the rising vapor, but she couldn't help herself. Inhaling through a tight circle between her lips, Golden worked the porridge around on her tongue amidst the cooling air until it was acceptable to swallow.

She exhaled with an audible gasp, and her jaw dropped, tongue still tingling. Golden abandoned the first bowl and moved on to the second. She didn't rush this time. Instead, she surveyed the porridge, relieved to find it steam-free. After scooping a level amount off the top to match the first, she blew on it first for good measure and then wrapped her lips around the spoon.

Her blue eyes flashed wide. Where the first bowl had been boiling, the second was frigid. Flavors of honey and apple were pleasing, yet because of the temperature, it had the consistency of strange ice cream. It congealed in her throat, and Golden managed to swallow the mass. Neither porridge was her preferred choice, but it felt great to have some food in her stomach.

Golden advanced to the third and final bowl. No steam rose from the porridge, and when she stuck the tip of her index finger into the middle, a pleasant warmth greeted her. "Okay. Last one." Confident the contents were neither too hot nor too cold, she withdrew a bit more from the bowl than before and ate.

Cinnamon, honey, and apple washed over her tongue, and pleasure rippled in her mouth as all three flavors burst in a glorious symphony. The texture was perfect, and warmth spread from her core until all her other extremities glowed, too. The porridge was heaven— the greatest meal she had ever tasted. Golden closed her eyes, delighting in every bite. She dipped her spoon again and again, each mouthful better than the last. She lowered her spoon, but this time, a loud screeching sound shattered her reverie as metal scraped ceramic.

She hadn't meant to devour the whole thing, yet an empty bowl stared up at her. Even the sides had been scraped clean. Swallowing, Golden dropped the spoon and stood. The room sloshed side to side. Stumbling, she tried to right herself and reached out to grab the table, but her palm missed the corner, and she crashed to the floor, slamming the side of her face on the edge on the way down. The tile greeted her with a harsh slap as her skull bounced. She put a hand to her head, groaning into the floor.

"What was that?"

Golden's speech slurred. Her tongue was a swollen root that seemed to germinate in her mouth. Blinking, she tried to clear her eyes of the sudden cloudiness, but her vision only worsened. She smeared the heel of her hand across her eyelids once more and climbed to her knees before straightening on her feet. Taking a shaky step forward, she held out her arms and tried to navigate through the dusky shadows. Maybe if she reached the front door and found the light again, her sight would return. It was just too dark in the decrepit house.

The soles of her flats scuffed across the floor. Golden tried to remember the distance from the kitchen to the foyer. Surely, she hadn't walked that far.

Snip. Snip.

A metallic bite echoed off the walls. Golden froze. It sounded like the crisp hiss of scissors. Her skin prickled with the sense that someone was watching her. Out of the corner of her eye, Golden caught a blond curl drifting through the air to where it landed beside her shoe. Another fell, twirling gracefully. She could only stare at the severed pieces. Slowly, she reached up and clutched the ends of her locks and found a sizeable chunk missing. Her heart pounded. Someone was in there with her. Close enough to cut her hair.

Spinning in a slow circle, Golden searched the dark angles of the expansive living room on her right for whoever was there, but her eyesight was too distorted. Up ahead, the front door called, a shining exit from the strange nightmare. She ran as fast as her impaired sight allowed, but then both halves of the open door slammed shut simultaneously, their silver locks sliding into place with cheerful clinks.

Unable to halt her momentum, Golden collided with the thick door. Her forehead smacked against the wood, and a pained yelp fell from her lips. Stifling her tears, she yanked on the handle with enough vigor to pull it off, but the door refused to budge under her onslaught. Next, she fumbled to locate the dead bolts. All she had to do was push them aside and she'd be free.

Reaching onto her tiptoes, she stretched her arm above her head in the direction she thought she had glimpsed them earlier, but her hand felt lumpy and stiff, as if she were losing control of its operation.

Snip. Snip.

The two sounds sent her heart racing as she struggled to find the lock. As she stretched her legs to search higher, her dress rode up and exposed her calves. With one hand, Golden secured her long hair in front of her chest. But her hair wasn't the scissors' target this time.

Snip.

Slicing into her Achilles tendon, the sharpened blades ripped the flesh asunder, withdrawing fast before her weight gave out and she crumpled to the floor.

Golden screamed. Her eyes bulged with pain and fear.

Pressing a hand to her wound, Golden pointed her foot

to keep from stretching the torn skin. Blood, warm and slippery, pulsed over her fingers. Without the sunlight from the previously open door, the darkness grew suffocating. She couldn't get out that way, and from her earlier inspection of the windows, she knew she would never be able to get one of them open. Her only chance now was to find a back door.

Snip. Snip.

The scissors whispered again but didn't touch Golden.

"Get away from me!"

The occupant was toying with her, and now she was an injured mouse for the cat to bat about. A feral shriek fell from Golden's mouth as she pushed herself onto her other leg. She hobbled only a few steps farther into the living room before the pain became too much. A steady flow of blood dripped down the curvature of her ankle and squished under her heel. She gripped the back of a low armchair for support, but the material was too soft. She couldn't maintain a firm enough grip. She let go, fearful her body would get sucked into the squishy frame.

Golden gritted her teeth and hopped again. This time, a small wooden chair positioned in the middle of the great room was her goal. If she managed to make it there, she could rest and work up the nerve to keep going. Baby steps.

Tears pooled in Golden's eyes and flowed onto her cheeks. The pain was indescribable. All she wanted to do was lie down and cry, but she knew whoever had cut her, stalked her flight.

One, two, three, four, five, six steps.

Golden shouted aloud as she dragged her injured leg. The little chair loomed closer. At last, her hand scraped the carved wood, and she threw all her weight onto the four legs. She exhaled a shaky breath, but she was too heavy, the chair too fragile. The narrow spindles gave out, came loose from the frame, and scattered onto the floor with hollow pings, like baby teeth knocked loose.

"No!"

Golden went down as the legs slipped and bucked the front of the chair off the floor. She landed hard on her elbow, and one of the jagged spindles pierced her side. Gripping the stake, she jerked it free, praying it hadn't pierced anything vital. Her scarlet stained fingers applied pressure to the gash as a strained wheeze emanated in the back of her throat. She fought to stand. Blood dripped loudly onto the floorboards, the flow too steady to be superficial. A husky chuckle ricocheted around the room, sounding impossibly large.

Golden curled a hand around the spindle's length, fingers knobby and thick. Her dexterity was laughable, but at least now she carried a weapon. Golden jabbed at the darkness, arms swinging wildly. "You stay away from me!"

Another bemused exaltation answered, and a massive shadow shifted near the foot of the staircase. Golden strained her eyes, able to identify a bright square of light. The back door or possibly another window. Her heart raced. She could make it.

A third chair and the one closest to the door waited, standing erect and sturdy. Golden's calf burned, muscles seizing with overuse. She hopped forward, stretching out her arm as her vision tunneled. Her destination seemed so far. Her torn tendon popped as her mauled ankle flopped uselessly, rotating around the joint. She had been reduced to a sack of bones and blood with one brush of the blades. Squeezing her eyes shut to staunch the pain blossoming in her side, Golden launched her body forward without care to cushion her injuries.

She knew her chances of survival were dwindling. She wasn't a fool. She was losing too much blood to exact this level of energy. Golden's head swam, growing foggy as her thoughts slowed. A few more minutes and the instinct to fight would leak out of her altogether, trailing on the floor with the rest of her essence.

The third chair's woven fabric grazed her fingertips, and a relieved sigh fell from her lips. This one didn't flinch under her touch and remained firm. It was a small comfort in the nightmare she had found herself drowning in, just right to bolster what little hope remained.

Golden did her best to calculate the distance to the swatch of light from her newest perch. Seven hops. The farthest she'd gone in one campaign yet. She hung her head and cursed the cloaked demon taunting her.

If only I hadn't left the trail.

The thought slunk into her mind, taking up immediate residence. Why had she veered from her plans? She was headed to the spring for a swim when she had smelled the porridge and the idea of a hot, scrumptious meal had carried her farther into the woods, like a spell or a drug.

The truth hit Golden like one of the sharp pinches Red would deliver to the tender skin on the back of her arm. The porridge, the house— it was all a trap designed to lure her into a secluded part of the forest where no one would see or even hear her pleas for help. She thought back to the three bowls. The way her head had swam after she ingested their contents. She licked her dry lips. The porridge was poisoned.

"You're a dull one, aren't you?" the shadow by the stairs said. Its voice was higher than Golden had anticipated, with a sweet yet gravelly melody. "But of course you are. What other type of human would venture into an abandoned home just for something to eat?"

"A hungry one," Golden replied through gritted teeth.

"Please, you've got sizeable meat on those bones. I think

you're greedy. A greedy little piggy." The shadow laughed in unison with the snip of the scissors.

"Why are you doing this?"

The speaker clucked her tongue. "Why else do you fatten up a piggy? For slaughter of course, you silly thing."

"Please," Golden begged. "Just let me go. I won't tell anyone. Just please—"

A guttural roar bellowed as the shadow leapt closer, remaining outside the sunlight illuminating the crimson puddles on the floor. "Stop the whining. It's very unattractive."

"Who are you?" Golden asked. She wiped her eyes in another futile attempt to clear them.

The shadow slid forward. The edge of a moss-green paisley dress fluttered into a sunray's touch. Golden strained her sight. The fabric looked like something her grandmother would don.

"We're no one in particular. A simple family with simple tastes. We've lived here for years, long before you and that noisy town was established. It's actually because of its foundation that we've had to alter our hunting practices. It's not as easy anymore. You humans and your guns. So instead, I devised a system in which our prey saunters right up to our doorstep. Only one meal ever managed to escape, but no one believed him, and my husband finished him off the next night. You remind me of Peter in a way."

Peter.

The name slammed around inside Golden's befuddled mind like a leaf caught in a maelstrom. The news of her father's death had hit her hard, but she couldn't say she was surprised. After weeks of sneaking out to the taverns and groping bar maids, she had assumed a jealous husband or angry bookie, fed up with her father's empty purse, had killed him. She recalled when the constable told Mama; his large paunch had barely fit beneath the kitchen table.

He'd spoken of finding her father's body near the edge of the woods a mile from their house. His intestines had been ripped from their casing and strewn about like cold noodles. His lower legs had been chewed off at the knees, femurs sticking out like a human kabob, while blood blasted nearby tree trunks. The police said his body must have been ravaged by wolves. Golden remembered his ravings the night before about spying a huge beast in the forest. Like everyone else, she'd dismissed it as another tall tale he'd crafted under the influence of ale to excuse his lateness upon return.

Now, Golden knew the truth. Her father had been lured to the house just as she was, but the wily bastard managed to get away, only to end up in their clutches the next day after his quest to drown his anxieties in pint after pint.

"He was my father," Golden said, her voice a whisper.

"Ah, I thought there was a resemblance. I hope you taste better. My husband said your father was far too bitter, but alcohol will do that to the organs."

"What are you?"

The sound of popping saliva answered as the shadow's lips stretched into a wicked grin. Yellowed fangs reflected the dim light, canines as long as Golden's thumb. Her breathing hitched as the rest of the creature materialized out of the darkness. The green dress stretched at least seven feet tall. Dark brown fur extended from capped sleeves, forearms ending in massive paws. The *snip-snip* of scissors tingled again, but Golden realized the shadow wasn't holding the presumed instrument. The sound— and the object that had cut her tendon— was the creature's thick claws. The monster tapped the ends together, mimicking the snap of scissors.

"Did it hurt when I cut you? It's always my favorite part. My husband and child are too rambunctious. They don't have the patience to wait, to stalk."

Golden's gaze continued up, and even with her blurry sight, the face that greeted her was terrifying. Dark brown fur covered the skull, and a shiny black nose was situated above smiling jaws. But her eyes . . . her eyes were obsidian pools that held not an ounce of mercy.

Golden gasped, her mouth trembling, "You're a bear."

"Very astute, child. Our numbers used to be great, but your hunters wiped out our kin. My family is the only one left, and we've made it our mission to eat as many of your kind as we can. Justice, you see."

"But I never killed one of you. Neither had my father. He wasn't a hunter, just a drunk and a cheat."

The bear shrugged and tapped her nails. "And my sister's cubs never harmed a human. Yet, they were butchered and flayed. Skins carved from their skeletons and turned into rugs!" Spittle flew from her lips and landed on Golden's cheek. "You and your kind are the true monsters. Killing for sport to hang our heads on your walls. So, we will devour you, piece by piece, delighting in every bite."

Golden lunged for the door, done listening and waiting to be eaten. One, two, three strides, but a thunderous cacophony rumbled behind her. The bear roared, darting after her. With one swipe of her large paw, her claws raked Golden's back, shredding fabric and flesh to curly red ribbons.

Golden screamed and stumbled. The force of the hit sent her crashing to the floor. Her back stung and her side exploded in pain as she landed on the wound from the spindle. Fresh tears rolled down her face over the salty tracks of the dried ones. Mama Bear leaned down and flipped Golden onto her back, digging a long claw into the raw gash on her side.

Golden's eyes bulged as warm blood welled to the surface, the pain blinding. White stars burst behind her eyes as the bear wiggled her claw, shredding whatever organ lay within reach.

"Stop!" Golden shouted. "Please stop!" She curled into the fetal position and swatted at the bear's arm with feeble strength.

"Are you done playing with me, child?" Mama Bear pouted. She withdrew her curved talon, her long pink tongue wrapped around the claw and licked Golden's blood like honey. A deep, satisfied groan emanated in the back of her throat.

"Leave me alone!" Golden sobbed. With one hand, she tried to pull her body across the floor. Mama Bear gripped the doorknob. Despite herself, hope inflated in Golden's chest. She didn't say anything more, just stared at her captor with pleading eyes. The knob turned with a heavenly click. Mama Bear pulled the door open, and cheerful rays of sunlight streamed in. She was letting Golden go! Maybe they wanted to chase her. Perhaps, her capture had been too easy. Whatever the reason, Golden didn't care. Anything would be better than dying on that floor without hope of ever being found.

"Baby Bear!" Mama Bear called.

Golden's breathing hitched, and the possibility of escape shattered.

"Lunchtime!"

PART II

Golden arched her back and twisted her neck to glimpse the child. The doorway remained empty, but the rhythm of little feet pounded through the yard. Then, a thick shadow fell across her face.

"There you are, sweetums," Mama Bear cooed. "Hungry?" She gestured to where Golden lay incapacitated on the floor. The cub let out an excited snarl. "Eat up, but save some for your father."

At his mother's words, the building tension popped. Launching his small frame across the threshold, Baby Bear dropped to all fours and raced forward. A scream caught in Golden's throat as the cub advanced with eyes dilated, jaws salivating, and tongue lolling between pointed teeth. She tried to turn, to get her leg up to protect herself against the furry bullet, but she was too weak.

Bracing herself for the impact, Golden inhaled a quick breath. Sun-kissed fur tickled her cheek. The scent transported her back home to when she and Red would run through the wildflower fields behind their cottage. Ghostly laughter accompanied the memory. What she wouldn't give to be back there. To hug her sister and apologize for letting their bond slip away.

Pain pierced her thoughts, and Golden seized as her consciousness slammed back to the present. Baby Bear's fangs closed around her shoulder and sunk into the thick flesh. Scarlet blood bubbled over his teeth, then exploded in a fountain as he tore open a vein, splattering the glass façade of the antique grandfather clock behind him.

Golden's muted screams finally broke free, creating an eerie harmony to Baby Bear's chewing. Beating on the cub's face with her fist, she struggled to get out from under his hold. Baby Bear growled, raspy and low. He sunk the tips of his claws into her thigh and the others into her chest to cement his grip on her.

"Stop!" Golden's sobs were ragged moans. She didn't have the energy to keep fighting. The pain was too great.

Baby Bear swallowed a warm mouthful of Golden's muscle and licked his muzzle clean. Golden looked down and caught a glimpse of her shredded shoulder and gasped. Raw tissue lay exposed beneath wet flaps of skin. Squiggly, pale red, and translucent veins splayed out like brittle pasta, severed in half, dripping blood down her forearm. A stump of humerus shone, teeth marks peppering the bone.

"That's enough now, dear. Why don't you take her up to your father?" Mama Bear smoothed the front of her apron and patted the fur on her cheeks. "I'll be up shortly. Just need to clean up this mess first."

Rancid breath the scent of copper, washed over Golden's face as Baby Bear exhaled, coating her in a cloud of hot vapor. He glanced at his mother, and for one horrifying moment, she feared he'd gnaw through her bone to take her entire arm.

The reality of what was to come was far worse.

Abandoning his post by Golden's head, Baby Bear jumped down the length of her body. In the same swift motion, he buried his teeth in her calf, securing his jaws around her uninjured leg. She tried to jerk free, but the moment he bit down, he began to pull, his destination the stairs. In crisp erratic movements, Golden was dragged backward, her weight doing little to impede his progress.

"No, no, no, no!" Golden reached out, searching frantically for anything to grab to halt her ascent. Blood smeared across the floor from her shoulder, and she saw the way Mama Bear shook her head with disappointment. Hopefully, it would delay another set of teeth from feasting on her for a few minutes.

Golden's fist wrapped around an ornate side table's narrow leg and her nails gouged the polished walnut. Baby Bear yanked her again, tossing his head side to side as he wrestled her around the banister like a dog with a toy. In response, her body snapped, toppling the furniture down on top of her ribcage. A porcelain vase depicting navy and white florals cracked and splintered, dousing her in lukewarm water. It reeked of damp earth and decay. Slimy stems slithered across her exposed neck and the unwelcome sensation caused her skin to prickle. An icy breath cooled her fevered flesh before her racing heart set her skin aflame once more.

"Please! Please tell him to stop!"

Golden didn't recognize her own voice. Her pleas were raspy and broken, her words guttural chaos spilling forth from cracked lips. Mama Bear simply smiled, venom in her gaze as her son crested the bottom step. His back claws curled around the wooden tread to gain the perfect leverage. Up and up he climbed, wrenching her back and forth at haphazard angles.

Golden did her best to protect her jaw and face from dragging atop the hard stairs with the back of her hand. Her chest smashed against the steps, tenderizing her skin even further. Her one hand snagged on a lower tread, and for one glorious moment, she could catch her breath. Above her, Baby Bear roared behind his teeth, ripping and yanking her leg with all his might to shake her grip loose. Another frustrated growl reverberated behind his teeth.

Mama Bear walked over with her paws crossed over her stomach. Bending at the waist, she brought her face level with Golden's. Her reserved demeanor flickered, offering a glimpse of the rage that burned beneath. "You're not being a very considerate house guest, my dear. I suggest you start using some manners or I'll ensure your demise lasts weeks." Before she finished speaking the last syllable, she flexed her claws and swiped Golden's hand from her wrist to her fingertips, carving three deep cuts in the thin tissue.

Golden cried out and involuntarily released her hold. Baby Bear tugged again, and she flew backward from the cub's overexertion. Her chin smacked the next riser, and her teeth rattled violently. Black spots bloomed across her vision as her body went limp from both pain and exhaustion. Maybe she should just let them kill her. She had no doubt Mama Bear would follow through with her threat. At least the first option would be quicker and less painful. A shooting ache sizzled up her leg as one of Baby Bear's teeth pinched a nerve. She let out an anguished sigh. Yes, death would be so much better than this.

The upstairs hallway slid by in a blur. Baby Bear pulled her past a closed door before turning and heaving her into a dark space, spitting out her leg and dropping her onto the floor. Golden wrinkled her nose and shivered. Her clothes were soaked from the overturned vase, and the room was doused in shadow, isolated from the sun's warming rays. She shook her head, trying to expel the scent of mold from her nostrils, but it held firm, growing stronger.

Golden rolled onto her side and cradled her head with her uninjured bicep, then stifled a scream. Lying beside her was a corpse. She couldn't tell if it was a man or a woman, for the flesh on the face was too badly decomposed. A moment later, the glassy eyeball moved, wriggling in the dry socket.

"Can you hear me?" Golden whispered, aghast they had managed to cling to life this long. The body reeked of death. She waited for the person to respond or blink, but their pointed stare endured. It was then that a thick fat maggot the color of spoiled milk emerged from behind the eyeball. Its rounded brown head swayed, mouth opening and closing.

Chunky gray lumps of half-digested porridge expelled over Golden's lips and hit the floor with a wet splash. Sick dribbled down her chin as she shimmied back, trying to put as much distance between her and the skeletal figure as possible. She'd thought the cub was bringing her to a dining room of sorts, but this was a boneyard.

Arching her neck, Golden scanned the room. Apart from the body next to her, she counted three additional skeletons, all in various stages of decomposition. The glaring similarity they shared was the lack of meat in the center. All of their chest cavities down to their torsos gaped, as if an animal had rooted around in their ribcages, eager to extract the juicy organs buried inside. She swallowed at the truth of her impression.

Golden held her breath and listened for any sign of the bears. She could hear only the heavy slap of the mop downstairs. Her deltoid must have satiated Baby Bear's hunger for the moment, and Papa Bear had yet to make an appearance. For the first time since entering the house, she was alone.

PART III

Pushing her hand beneath her, Golden managed to lift her weight off the floor and sit up. She gripped a steel bar behind her head and pulled herself to her feet. Bright pain coursed through her half-eaten calf, but she refused to stop. If she did, she'd be one of the maggot-filled husks that littered the floor.

The door to her prison cell stood slightly ajar, and a halo of soft light rimmed the dark frame. Hobbling forward, Golden flinched at her staggered gait, terrified of calling attention to herself. She clutched the wall and put her faith in the lath and plaster to keep her upright. Skirting the threshold, Golden exited into the hallway. The first open door revealed a small bed, but the room was too filthy to discern anything besides the ragged animal skins that covered every surface. Tufts of fur littered the floor in large clumps of red, black, and gray. She shivered as she imagined the frightened screams of the poor animals Baby Bear had disemboweled. She knew firsthand what it felt like to be his plaything.

Golden moved farther down and crept past the second door. A massive shape crouched over a hidden object, its shoulders bucking and rolling as it pulled at something level with its waist. It moved again and a hollow popping sounded, like a stubborn joint finally releasing. The monster arched backward and tossed its large head to the ceiling. A human arm flew into the air, fingertips brushing the dark timber beams above.

Golden stifled a yelp and slapped her hand over her mouth. Papa Bear. He caught the severed appendage by the wrist and folded the fingers between his teeth with his paw. The crunch of bone vibrated in the pit of her stomach. She knew it was another victim, but it wasn't clear how much of them was left. Dark maroon-stained sheets hung to the floor like a macabre waterfall, but the dim lighting made it too dark to determine how fresh the bear's tastes leaned. The giant growled and shifted his stance, twisting toward the hall.

Golden spun and lightly landed against the wall. She exhaled a shaky breath. There was no way she could navigate the stairs with her injuries, but maybe there was a window she could jump from. Keeping her back pressed to the wall, she inched farther down the hallway. No window stood vigil at the end like in her home, but maybe one of the other rooms would present an opportunity.

Two doors still lingered. Biting the inside of her cheeks, Golden considered both. The space beneath the door of the one farthest away glowed brighter and offered her the best chance to discover a working window. She's taken a labored step when the bottom stair groaned. She froze in place as a choir of growls announced Baby Bear. Mama was quick to answer his unidentifiable mumblings.

"You put her in the pantry? I told you to take her straight to Papa's room." Mama Bear sighed, and her footsteps climbed higher. "In that case, you can probably have some more. I doubt he's finished with the hiker yet, anyway."

Garbled excitement replied. They were getting closer. Golden heard the puff of Mama's breath slip between her teeth. Panicked, she snuck through the closest door just as the tip of their claws raked the landing, having no choice but to leave the door open lest they see or hear it close. Breathing wide through her mouth, she tried to navigate the jumbled mass of broken furniture that buried the floor beneath her. The rubble appeared to be chair legs, all splintered and cracked like extracted ribs tossed this way and that. The haphazard layout was a minefield of lethal avenues. One wrong step and she'd be impaled on wooden fangs.

Why do they have so many?

Her eyes went wide as her fingers gingerly touched the hole in her side. The spindles at her feet were the same that had pierced her flesh downstairs, and Golden envisioned the Bear family setting the same trap repeatedly. The isolated house, the porridge, and the rickety chair. Add in an endless parade of ignorant travelers and the ruse practically ran itself. Cue a few prodding slashes from Mama and the bears could exact their revenge and fill their bellies without ever leaving the house.

Dragging her leg, Golden edged toward the window, but upon first touch her heart plummeted. Years of dust and grime smothered her fingers. Applying as much pressure as she could, she pushed up on the latch, but it was stuck tight. The panes rattled mockingly.

The squeak of a hinge disturbed the tension. Mama and Baby Bear had reached the pantry of bones. A quick sweep of the rotting corpses would confirm her glaring absence. Heart racing, Golden surveyed the wreckage of the room. Leaning in the right corner was a dilapidated mattress. Rust colored splotches soaked the material, no doubt from a decade's worth of feasts. She gagged, unable to keep the revulsion down.

Watery bile filled her cheeks and coated her tongue. Hunching over, Golden spat the sick into the corner. It dribbled down a nearby chair leg and puddled in a sour mess. Down the hall, two loud roars erupted. Her wardens knew she was gone.

"Where is she?"

Doors slammed and harsh growls emanated from down the hall.

"No, she didn't come down. I would have seen!"

Amidst the commotion and out of time, Golden dove beneath the concaved mattress. It had lost its form long ago. Flattening her body, she lay down and twisted her spine to camouflage amongst the rest of the debris. Hurried footsteps stomped across the hall.

"Do you have her?"

A deep baritone answered. The tone was too low for Golden to distinguish any words through the walls.

"The girl. The one with the honey-colored hair. The one you saw in the woods and told me to catch. *That girl.*"

Another thick rumble sounded.

"Then put that down and help me search!"

Golden flinched as heavy paws pounded floorboards. The house shook as it sounded like one of the bears collided with the hallway wall. She hunched down even lower in her hiding spot as her teeth sawed her bottom lip. The house was sizeable, but Mama Bear knew Golden was sequestered somewhere upstairs. To say she had minutes left was generous.

Growls filled the air, along with the quick tempo of running paws. A small hunched shape raced past the open door. Baby Bear was on his way to investigate the bright room at the end of the hall. Golden's teeth clacked together. She wished she had closed the door behind her. The simple plank of thin wood would have offered a sliver of cover.

Golden couldn't bask in the relief of Baby Bear's chosen direction, for in the next breath, Papa Bear lumbered in and smacked the door panel with enough force that it ricocheted off the interior wall and bounced back, hitting his muscular shoulder. Her blood ran cold when she caught sight of his face.

Peeking between a tangle of wooden legs, Golden was shocked to see the difference between him and the rest of the sleuth. Where Mama and Baby had smooth rich fur, Papa resembled a distorted carrion. Deep scars raked his features, carving the once tawny fur in three distinct bald patches across his face. Half his nose was missing, and the skinned hide surrounding it was gnarled and red— a combination of poorly healed wounds and remnants of his interrupted meal.

Golden flinched as his long pink tongue lolled out and licked the last few crimson droplets. The skin was shiny and blistered. She imagined a terrible fight with a brave hunter, fire and claw clashing in a fierce battle. She liked to think it was her father who had scarred the beast, attacking as best he could until his final breath, but the truth of his death was far less heroic. He was nothing more than a stumbling drunk with overconfidence that his proximity to town would keep him safe. One look at Papa Bear and she knew one heft of his mighty paw would have knocked her father unconscious. He made an easy snack.

Her gaze traveled up the great animal. Puckered skin rippled around his right eye, scrunching the flesh in a tight knot and seemingly minimizing his sight line. Hope flickered in her chest, ridiculously persistent. If her predator's senses were impaired, maybe she could evade his detection.

Papa Bear grunted and expelled hot breath from his nostrils. He turned, maneuvering one paw across the other as he exited the room. Behind him, Mama Bear padded to a halt. Guttural growls emanated from her throat, and her eyes were bright with fury. Papa tossed his head as he delivered the bad news. A great bellow fell from Mama's jaws, and the sides of her cheeks quivered with the volume. Golden didn't understand how her scent had evaded them. Maybe the house was so saturated with the smell of blood and exposed tissue that they couldn't identify one body from another. Mama and Baby Bear ran downstairs in a frantic panic.

Papa Bear followed behind and had taken two deliberate steps away when his gait paused. Lifting his head, he sniffed the still air, the end of his ravaged nose twitching. With a groan, he rose to his hind legs and walked back into the debris-filled room. His mouth opened, and thunderous grunts boomed in the back of his throat. His heavy footsteps sent several of the discarded chair legs shifting in a small avalanche of movement. Golden didn't move and sent up a silent prayer that the threadbare mattress could withstand the vibration.

She swallowed the growing lump in her throat. What had changed? The blood from her shoulder was starting to congeal, and she had sustained no new wounds to spark fresh interest. Still, Papa Bear stormed closer, brushing broken spindles and arm rests to the side in a clattering tidal wave. That's when she remembered her vomit in the corner. The putrid aroma of acids and bile stood out like a glowing neon sign amongst the copper-scented blood soaking the floorboards.

Papa Bear's rasping articulations grew louder as his paw swung back and forth to clear a path to accommodate his girth. The force of his movements knocked a few spindles loose and sent them careening in Golden's direction. One skittered beneath the mattress and bit her cheek. Without thought, she sucked in a sharp breath. The skin broke, and warm blood oozed down her face.

Papa stopped and huffed with anticipation. He scooped the makeshift barrier away from his prize. Golden lay there, helpless to save herself as he grunted with victory. She fumbled for the bloody stick of wood beside her thigh, and with shaking fingers, she grasped the shard, clutching it in her fist with the jagged edge facing her enemy. It wasn't much more than a toothpick Papa could use to clean his teeth with after, but it was a small comfort to not be totally defenseless.

He grabbed the side of the mattress in his jaws and threw it across the room. Warping in the air, it bounced off the wall, then collapsed in on itself in a crumpled heap. Papa Bear whipped his head back, his beady onyx eyes alive with hunger, and sunk to all fours once more. He bellowed and lunged, his teeth dripping with saliva. Golden screamed in unison and thrust upward. She closed her eyes, pressing even harder when her weapon sunk into the jellylike disc of his eyeball. Watery liquid squirted from the puncture, spraying her raised chin as Papa howled and swatted the intrusive object away. Golden released her hold and scuttled backward out of range of his lethal claws. Hitting the floor with a hollow ping, the spindle rolled to the side, the tip glistening with translucent juice. Squeezing his injured eye shut, Papa Bear roared, the sound a deafening blast.

Golden's shoulder blades bumped the plaster behind her once she'd consumed the last of her space to retreat. Papa Bear fixed her with a murderous glare as footsteps echoed down the corridor. The rest of the family was coming to witness her last breaths. She opened her mouth to whisper a final plea, but Papa didn't extend such a curtesy.

In one powerful leap, he plunged his claws into Golden's

chest, carving her shirt and tissue with minimal effort. Her eyes bulged, and a volatile cry climbed her throat. The sound didn't escape her lips, however. Papa thrust his head closer, clutched her neck between his fangs, and ripped the thin flesh. Scarlet ribbons of blood pulsed out as he reared back, chewing a large flap of skin. Exposed veins and raw muscle shone wetly. Golden wheezed, her torso twisting as the involuntary instinct of flight battled shock. Papa swallowed, then indulged in another bite, his teeth sliding through the warm tissue like cotton candy.

The second bite went deeper and exposed a column of white spine. Without the support of her neck, Golden's head tipped forward, her chin coming to rest on her collarbone as her final breath leaked from agape lips. Her bright blue eyes grew foggy with death's billowing shroud.

Mama and Baby Bear ran into the room.

"Thank goodness," Mama said. "She was a crafty one. More persistent than I thought."

Papa nodded and stepped back, licking his muzzle clean.

"Go on, Baby. You did such a nice job helping me search the house."

Bounding ahead, Baby Bear placed his paw on Golden's forehead and pushed up, revealing the delicacy beneath. Contented sighs filled the room as he nuzzled chunks of fresh meat. Blood continued to drip, soaking the ends of Golden's hair and saturating the once beautiful strands to muddy rust. Mama Bear brushed her son to the side, ready to take her turn at last.

She bit into the shoulder Baby Bear had tenderized downstairs and moaned as the warm muscle and blood washed over her tongue. The mop still needed wringing; a pot of porridge simmered on the stove; the plot of nightshade needing tending; and Baby's broken chair pieces littered the living room. But all that could wait. She was tired, and right now, her only desire was to lose herself in her hard-earned meal, for revenge was truly delicious.

The End

The nursery rhyme, "Do you know the Muffin Man?" is a childhood staple that many parents sing to their infants and toddlers. I always pictured a jovial baker whipping up delicious muffins in his small bakery at the end of Drury Lane. It wasn't until a few months ago, however, that I learned about a possible grisly truth behind that cheerful song.

Scrolling through social media one day, I saw a video by Jack Willamson claiming that the Muffin Man was a real person and the world's first serial killer. His name was Frederic Thomas Lynwood and between 1589 and 1598, it is rumored that he murdered approximately fifteen children by luring them into dark alleys with a muffin tied to a string, and seven pastry chefs with a sharpened wooden spoon, while living on Drury Lane in London, England.

The song itself was said to be created to warn other children to stay away from Drury Lane, lest they want to meet their demise by the baker. Although these claims have remained unproven, it is a fascinating urban legend that inspired my own reimaging of this classic rhyme.

Perhaps it is just a scary story that evolved over the years in response to Drury Lane's sour reputation as the "worse street in London," or maybe there really was a killer baker who targeted the hungry children living on the streets. The truth may never be known, but if there is any fact to the rumors, the following story is what I envisioned life must have been like living amidst his reign of terror.

Enjoy.

Dapcevich, Madison. (2021, February 12). *Was 'Muffin Man' Song a Warning to Kids About 16th-Century Serial killer?* Snopes. http://snopes.com/fact-check/muffin-man-song-serial-killer

CAYTLYN BROOKE

DOWN ON DRURY LANE

CHAPTER 1

Tony bit the inside of his cheek until his teeth deformed the smooth flesh. He didn't want to do this, but *his* stomach wasn't the only one that would be empty if he chickened out. With a grime-filled fingernail, he flicked an errant splinter on the empty stall's column. The sharp bite pierced the sensitive skin far below the keratin. Tony eyed the farmer's wagon across the narrow alleyway. Juicy Honey Crisp apples, Anjou pears, plump peaches, and ripe oranges decorated the crates and spilled out of the tops of metal pails. A glistening temptation.

The crowd had thickened. Maids gathered their mistresses' breakfasts for the moment they awoke, chefs combed the stalls for the freshest produce, and mothers enjoyed their one moment of peace to collect the day's milk and bread before their husbands sequestered themselves at the office until nightfall and the children drained every last morsel of energy from their veins, only to repeat it all again tomorrow.

Tony sawed his tongue between his teeth and wondered if he could slice off the little bumps he had seen reflected at him in the darkened windows of the abandoned warehouse where they slept. Old Man McGinty prowled around his cart and hawked his fruits. His eyes lingered on every person in the alleyway, likely analyzing if they were a prospective buyer or a simple meanderer not worth his time.

Tucked away beyond the far corner, Tony knew Juliette and Miles awaited his signal, but still he hesitated. They targeted Old Man McGinty because he was near blind in one eye and couldn't walk without his cane, but he was nasty. If he caught anyone thieving from his stall, the old man wouldn't hesitate to cut off a hand and leave the perpetrator in the street to bleed out. The incident three weeks ago was branded into Tony's memory.

Cassandra, another orphan who'd often snuggled with their crew when the nights grew particularly cold, had tried to pinch an orange from McGinty. She'd almost succeeded, when upon her retreat, she tripped over his cane and collapsed at his feet. Before she could blink, the old man had withdrawn a serrated kitchen knife from the sheath at his waist, wrenched her arm up, and swung the blade across the inside of her freckled wrist. The blade had cut through the tendons and nerves with ease and severed her hand in one practiced slice.

Cassandra's arm had fallen to her chest with a dull thud as the stump squirted blood into her incredulous eyes. The orange released from her fingers and rolled over the cobblestones. The rind made a sickening squelch as it traversed the growing puddle of blood, leaving tiny imprints atop the worn rocks.

McGinty had cleaned the knife on his sleeve and re-sheathed it before wiping his nose with the back of his hand, then bent down to retrieve the stolen fruit. He rubbed the blood off the rind and polished it on his shirt. The peel was slightly discolored in spots, but he placed it back on top of the display. The attempted heist and mutilation had taken only a minute and a half.

McGinty had pocketed Cassandra's bloody hand in his yellowed apron with a snicker and sent the toe of his heavy boot into her gut. "Git goin', little scum. If I see ya round here again, I'll take a leg next."

A maid passed by the gruesome scene, her pert nose held aloft, as if Cassandra's stench might infect her like a clinging virus. "I need three oranges, sir." She held her full basket in the crook of her elbow and refused to lower her gaze to the bleeding orphan sprawled underfoot.

"Beautiful morning, isn't it, ma'am?" McGinty said with a tip of his cap.

The maid pursed her lips. "On the contrary, it's a bit foul for my taste."

McGinty grinned and kicked Cassandra again. Another squeal of pain resounded as the young girl curled in on herself to protect her hollow stomach and the mangled stump from more trauma, and her complexion paled to a dangerous hue.

"Tell ya what, I'll give ya two peaches on the house. Freshly picked. A lil treat for yourself."

The maid glanced at the plump fruit out of the corner of her eye. She replied with a curt nod, then tucked the purchased fruit into the basket, taking great care to hide the delicate peaches away. She deposited two coins into McGinty's grubby palm and pivoted, careful to swish her long skirts away from the blood soaking the road, and snapped her dress over Cassandra's crumpled form.

After the maid's departure, Tony had run over from where he watched and hooked his thin arms beneath Cassandra's armpits to drag her out of reach of the cruel farmer. He'd hoped to be gone before McGinty dropped the charming salesman act, but he was too slow. Heavy fists rained down upon Tony's emaciated shoulders.

"Bleeding scum! Don't let me catch ya pilfering from me again!"

Tony hunched, tears leaking from his eyes as he pulled Cassandra's weight over the wet cobblestones. One of McGinty's blows caught him in the ear, threatening to send both him and his friend tumbling to the ground as he fought to keep his balance.

At last, Tony reached the corner, too far for the old man who wouldn't leave his wares unattended. Juliette and Miles sprang to action once McGinty had given up the chase and each carried one of Cassandra's legs. They headed to the nearby aid shelter, but the wound wasn't clotting. Bright red liquid spilled out of her body at an alarming rate. She grew cold in their arms and had died at some point between the alley and Truman Park.

The trio looked around. Dozens of people milled about the streets and paid the children as much mind as the garbage in the gutter. With little choice and heavy hearts, they carried Cassandra to a skeletal tree that stood isolated a few yards from the road. They'd lowered her body against the trunk and did their best to arrange her arms peacefully across her chest but could do nothing to hide the scarlet blood. Juliette's hands shook as she reached out and closed the young girl's dull eyes. None of them said anything. The market was about to close, and they still hadn't managed to pinch any food. They walked back, hoping against hope that the undertaker wandered by before the street dogs found Cassandra.

Tony hadn't slept that night, too terrified to shut his eyes. Yet there he was, just weeks removed from the nightmare, about to risk his life for their next meal. He steadied his quaking hands and stepped forward.

Tony wove in and out of the bustling alley and spied his approaching target. He'd seen the woman and her unruly children before. It was barely nine in the morning and already the mother carried the tangible weight of exhaustion and defeat like a yoke about her shoulders. He counted four kids, plus an infant balanced on her hip. What would two more be in the chaos?

As the woman and her brood passed their hiding place, Tony gave a subtle nod to Juliette and Miles. Not wasting any time, his friends slipped into the melee and positioned themselves around the mother like two moons falling into orbit. The family was almost parallel to McGinty's cart. Guilt formed in the pit of Tony's stomach for what he was about to do, but it rang with a hollow echo. Hunger outweighed the regret. Dropping his shoulder, he broke into a sprint and slammed into the woman's elbow that was wrapped around her one-year-old.

"Bleeding Christ!" the mother yelled as her grip gave way. She fumbled to right herself as Tony's unexpected hit threw her off balance along the jagged stones. The baby's shrill cry blared like a copper's siren as he hit the street, ruddy cheeks bright red with rage. The mother caught herself on the edge of the cart and sent forth an avalanche of apples.

"Bullocks!" McGinty hollered, rising from his wooden stool.

The children swarmed. Some helped their mother, while the others grabbed the runaway fruit as if each one was a shiny new toy. Tony froze with a terrified look on his face.

"I'm so sorry. I didn't mean to hit you." Tony stooped down to the dirty stones and picked the thrashing baby up by the waist.

"Git your filthy hands off 'im!" With the help of her two eldest children, the woman regained her balance. "Give 'im 'ere, you nasty gutter snake."

"I'm sorry. I— I—"

The mother ripped the child out of Tony's hands.

Out of the corner of his eye, he caught Juliette crying next to the woman's three-year-old. Her tears seemed genuine, but her hands were busy pocketing several apples into the hidden panel lining her coat. Miles stood amongst the two older children, watching with wide eyes against the stall. Without taking his eyes off the scene, his arm snaked behind him to collect a trio of oranges.

A firm hand secured Tony's upper arm as McGinty caught hold of him. In his other hand, he wielded his cane and brought it down with a furious thwack upon Tony's collarbone. A burst of pain exploded beneath his skin, causing him to cry out.

"Please! It was an accident, I swear!"

"Accident my arse. I'll teach ya to knock into people and send their goods flying off into the street." McGinty raised his cane once more and wrenched it back to deliver another cracking blow, but the mother threw her arm out to halt the attack.

"Enough of that. Surely, clumsiness doesn't warrant a dislocated shoulder. And here I thought you might'a been ready to defend me, but all you's worried about is yer precious pears and apples getting bruised."

She secured her baby back onto her hip and grabbed the fallen fruit out of the offering hands of her children, including Juliette. With a vengeance, the woman tossed fruit after fruit at McGinty who fumbled them with an ashen look on his face. He managed to catch a few, but most of them bounced off his barrel chest and hit the gravel below with a mushy plop.

"Come on, kids. Let's leave the farmer to his hawking."

Juliette and Miles blended in with the large brood, their inner pockets bulging with contraband. Tony slipped away amidst McGinty's juggling act, unwilling to be caught alone. He rounded the corner into an adjacent alleyway and circled back to their meeting place behind a dumpster. He exhaled a shaky breath and propped his weight against the brick wall. He tried to roll his shoulder, but the movement sent a fiery spike of pain through his upper chest. At least it wasn't broken. Tony frowned. He'd have a nasty bruise by day's end.

Miles and Juliette slunk into view a few moments later. The second they caught a glimpse of Tony, they broke into an excited run.

"We did it!" Juliette called.

"Mate, look at all this. Spoils of war!" Miles opened his coat to reveal his cache. A torrent of vibrant colors flashed. He'd nicked enough oranges, apples, and pears to last them a week. Juliette emptied her pockets as well, adding even more to the stolen feast, and they giggled like the children they were for the first time in months.

"That was a great plan, Tony," Miles said, patting him on the shoulder.

Tony winced and pulled down his stained collar. An angry red welt stood out starkly against his pale skin.

"Tony!" Juliette gasped as her smile wavered. "Are you all right?"

Tony shrugged nonchalantly, doing his best to dismiss his friends' sudden concern. "I'll be fine. McGinty landed a good shot, but I'll be right again in a few days. What should we eat first?" He swallowed the pain and tried to reclaim the gay excitement that had permeated the alley only moments ago.

"This orange has been calling my name since Tuesday," Miles said and grabbed the nearest fruit. His grimy fingernails sliced into the rind, then ripped into the vulnerable flesh within. The strong scent of citrus stung Tony's nostrils and made him salivate.

"I want an apple." Juliette held her chosen meal in her palms like the Holy Grail.

"Pass me a pear. I haven't had one since my mum . . ." Tony caught the oblong fruit and bounced it between his hands. He hadn't always been an orphan on the streets, but with each winter, his frost-covered fingertips and inescapable shivers made it more and more difficult to recall the memory of the life he'd had before he lost his mother.

Tony brought the pear to his lips, and his teeth pierced its cold skin, overwhelming his taste buds with nostalgia. A comfortable silence settled over the small group as they savored their hard-won meal. The fruit would only last for so long before they had to find carbs and protein; otherwise, they'd be clutching their guts with the runs— a lesson they had learned the hard way.

Tomorrow would bring new challenges, but tonight, their bellies were placated. They were alive for one more day.

CHAPTER 2

"We should at least check it out, Tony," Juliette repeated.

Miles punched his shoulder gently. "Yeah, come on, Tone. James let it slip that this guy just gives them away for free."

Tony stamped his feet against the frigid morning's bite and stuffed his hands in his pockets, hoping to discover a burst of hidden warmth, but only cold fabric grazed his fingertips. It wasn't that he hadn't heard of Drury Lane. The other street kids had been trading rumors about it for the last two days. Free food, as much as you could eat, and not the usual gruel the hotel kitchens sometimes collected for them. Instead, trays and trays of golden-brown muffins apparently awaited them, practically stacked to the sky. Tales of delicious aromas of banana, oatmeal raisin, and blueberry swirling in the air had reached their ears, sounding like a dreamlike escape from the stench of London's gutters. He'd even heard gossip that one day the muffins had contained chocolate chips— *real* chocolate, gooey and sweet in every bite. But Tony wasn't convinced. There was a catch. There had to be. No one in their right mind would feed a bunch of street kids for free. They were worse than cats.

"Who is this guy? Does anyone know?"

Miles shrugged. "Who cares. He's giving away free food."

Juliette chewed the raw skin around her cuticle and drew blood. "They call him the Muffin Man. How dangerous can he be?"

Tony pursed his lips and mulled over her words. It seemed too good to be true.

"Come on, Tone," Miles urged. "What other prospects do we have? We've got one orange to last the three of us till tomorrow. What's the harm in checking it out?"

Juliette nudged him with her elbow. "None of the kids I've talked to have gotten sick."

Tony emitted a weak laugh. Juliette was so perceptive.

"Okay, we'll head over tomorrow morning, but we stick together, and at the first sign of trouble we—"

"We're gone. We got it, mate." Miles clapped him on the back and let out a loud howl.

Juliette's breathy laughter joined, and Tony's stern countenance cracked into a crooked grin. Unease gnawed at his gut, but even he had to admit, the possibility of a warm treat for breakfast was hard to pass up.

Dawn crested with an unforgiving chill. Tony huddled beneath the threadbare blanket he had constructed from a burlap sack. The cold licked his exposed ankles where his shortening pants pulled away. Beside him, Juliette stirred and burrowed closer into his torso, chasing the little warmth he radiated. The space on the other side of Tony was empty, and the hollowness invited in the icy morning far earlier than he was prepared for.

The edge of their makeshift tent rippled, and the blue tarp crunched as the flap pulled back. Miles stuck his dark head into the shelter, his nose already red from exposure. "Get up, you fat sacks. The muffins will be gone at this rate!" He tossed the flap back wider, and a burst of cold air sent a wave of shivers along Tony's arms and slithered beneath his loose shirt.

"Aye! Shut it, would ya? I'm up."

Juliette groaned and yanked the thin blanket up under her chin. "Miles, stop it." Her muted whine rumbled as she pressed her face into Tony's side.

"Come on," he replied. "We have to get to Drury Lane. We agreed."

"He's right." Tony gritted his teeth and stood, gently sliding Juliette's head off his body. "Come on, Jules."

Begrudgingly, Juliette pushed the blanket off with an exasperated shove and drew her knees to her chest. "Give me a minute to change, then."

Tony nodded and grabbed his thin jacket before he slipped out of the tarp's incision to join Miles outside. The older boy bounced on the balls of his feet. Either he was trying to keep warm or his excitement made it physically impossible to remain still. Tony plunged his arms into the cool sleeves of his jacket. "She's getting dressed."

Miles snickered and hooked his hands in his pockets. "What's it matter? It's not like she has clean rags."

"Lay off her, mate. It gives her some control over our pitiful existence."

Miles shifted his stance and glanced down the alleyway. The bricks that towered above them changed from black to light orange as the sun stretched over the bordering buildings. He sucked his chapped lips. "Well, our pitiful existence is about to get a lot worse if she makes us miss a warm breakfast."

"Calm down. She'll be along."

The minute the words were out of Tony's mouth, the flap rippled, and Juliette emerged. A fresh, long-sleeved checkered shirt decorated her torso, and a black winter cap covered her head down to her eyebrows.

"Fast enough, Miles?"

Tony hid his snicker and inclined his head, gesturing to the right, where the mouth of the alley yawned. Together they hurried off, hesitant expectation guiding them forward.

CHAPTER 3

The trio smelled their destination before they reached the final turn. The rich aroma of sugar and rising flour propelled their feet faster. It was real. Tony hadn't taken Miles seriously, but the chilling wind confirmed he was awake instead of dreaming and, even better, closing in on their destination.

The soles of their shoes slapped the crumbling concrete, and Drury Lane opened like the Garden of Eden before them. A dozen kids stood along a brick wall. Tony glanced down the alleyway, but his search was fruitless and produced only festering dumpsters and steaming sewer drains. Where were the muffins? He sidled up to a kid with greasy black hair, half covered by a dingy wool cap. He nudged the younger boy with his elbow.

"What gives? We heard some guy was passing out breakfast."

The boy pointed to a rusted green door tucked behind a dumpster. "We're early. He comes out right at six. But it's a good thing you're here now, 'cause once he runs out, that's it till tomorrow."

"For a second, I thought my friend was pulling my leg," Tony said.

The kid's eyes bulged. "No, he's real. I've come two days in a row. He gives out everything he makes, but the bigger kids pushed me down yesterday and took all mine. I still got one that had been stepped on." His eyes raked Tony's tall stature. "You'll be okay, though. You're big."

Tony leaned against the cold bricks. He didn't acknowledge the kid's plight. That's how life was on the streets. "How does he pass them out? Is there a mad dash?" He imagined a mob of kids charging the alley and frowned. He'd seen a stampede firsthand. It wasn't pretty.

"This early, it's calm. We stay in line, but as the muffins run out, it starts to get tense. That's why I got pushed."

Tony studied the closed door. "Has anyone ever gone in there?"

The boy shook his head. "Door is locked. I don't think he has an actual shop, just an oven."

Tony furrowed his brow. Why would a man spend all his time baking for a bunch of orphans? Maybe he was simply a good person, but if life on the streets had taught Tony anything, it was that deep down, people were greedy selfish monsters who only cared about helping themselves. An overwhelming sense of foreboding gripped him. The whole situation was too good to be true. There had to be a catch.

A door hinge squealed. The gathered crowd moved as one as their conversations fell away. Miles and Juliette appeared at Tony's elbow.

"Let's go." Miles's eyes shone with anticipation.

The dozen or so kids stood quietly, waiting. From their vantage point, Tony and his friends caught sight of a short man wearing a stained hat that could have been white at one point in time. A bottle brush mustache stretched beneath his nose atop long thin lips. His eyes were the lightest blue Tony had ever seen, like a sheet of frosted ice threatening to crack. Shivers pierced Tony's spine, and a resonance of unease prickled in the back of his mind for a reason he couldn't pinpoint.

"Good morning." The Muffin Man's voice was high and nasally. "Is anyone hungry this fine day?"

A deafening chorus shouted in reply. The cacophony of voices bounced off the metal scaffolding that clung haphazardly to the brick structures. The Muffin Man raised the tray in his hands. Tony's mouth watered as tendrils of steam swirled in the frosty morning air, accompanied by the heady scent of cinnamon and raisin. He took a step closer.

"Excellent. I have prepared five trays. Form a line and everyone will receive three muffins. If there are more left over, we'll form another line for seconds."

As one, the children coalesced in a serpentine formation. No one pushed or argued. The promise of food was too great. Anxious feet shuffled the line forward. Tony, Miles, and Juliette fell in behind the kid with the greasy hair, and Miles glanced over his shoulder every few seconds.

"What are you looking at?" Juliette asked.

"I want to make sure no one else gets here."

"Seriously? Be grateful for the three you'll already get rather than trying to figure out more ways to stuff your face." Juliette huddled deeper into her scarf and blew warm air on the tips of her fingers.

Only two kids separated them from a warm breakfast now. Tony swallowed. A pulling sensation hooked in his gut and tugged toward his spine. Something told him they shouldn't be there, but the hollow echo of his stomach gnawing away at itself kept him rooted in place. He shook his head. He was being paranoid.

Around them, moans of pleasure swelled as the kids first in line bit into their prizes. Some children savored every bite, while others tore into them like rabid hounds and devoured every crumb in seconds. They seemed content, unsuspicious, and unbothered. Why then couldn't Tony shake his apprehension?

The greasy haired boy stepped before the Muffin Man. His fingers worried the tattered cuffs of his coat.

"Hello, young man. How are you today?" the Muffin Man asked with a wide smile.

Tony frowned, disliking the flash of the man's skeleton. His grin was far too wide, as if his true nature struggled to be concealed by the fleshy mask.

"Good," the boy answered. He fiddled a loose string on his sleeves between two grimy nails, appearing fearful, as if the Muffin Man were about to pull a cruel prank and deny him food for his empty belly.

The Muffin Man leaned down and presented the tray to the youth. "Which ones look good?"

The boy licked his lips and pointed to the three golden tops lining the corner of the pan. "Those please."

"Good choice, young sir." The Muffin Man hooked his forefinger and thumb into the edge of each depression and popped out the desired muffins. The boy accepted his treasures and nodded in thanks. He turned to leave, but the baker stopped him. "Here son, take one more." He reached into the deep folds of his apron and presented him with a smaller muffin. "Don't tell the others, but that's the only one with chocolate chips today." He winked, his bristly mustache twitching.

The boy took the gift in silence and smiled at the Muffin Man. He spun and exited the line to the right, the warm treat already kissing his lips. Tony caught his eye, but the boy glanced away and hurried off, shielding his spoils from prying eyes. No matter how friendly they'd been earlier, the kid wasn't about to risk losing his few extra bites.

"Next."

Miles shoved him from behind, bringing Tony's attention back around.

"Hi," he muttered.

"How are you this morning?"

Tony clenched his fists at his sides. The man was a robot—head, neck, and teeth all moving and clacking with a precision and rigidity that evoked a coldness that seemed to go undetected by the other children.

"Fine."

The Muffin Man flashed his eerie grin again. "Excellent. Which ones look good to you?"

Tony shook his head. "It doesn't matter."

The baker blinked. "In that case, take these three." He hooked his finger into the cups and popped a trio of muffins out in rapid succession. He handed them to Tony, his strange eyes nothing more than glassy marbles for all the feeling they reflected.

"Thank you." Tony caught the muffins and moved out of line to wait for Miles and Juliette. Their exchanges with the Muffin Man were identical to his own.

With breakfast in hand, the friends found a quiet spot to settle. While they'd waited, more children arrived and depleted any hope they might have harbored for seconds.

Miles's back hit the brick wall, and he slid down to the pavement. He raised one of the muffins to his mouth and took a large bite. "Ah, this is amazing. What'd I tell ya, mate?"

Juliette bit into hers as well and closed her eyes. "Whoa. I can't remember the last time I tasted something so good, and it's warm to boot." She took another bite and looked at Tony. His muffins sat untouched. "What's wrong? Why aren't you eating?"

Tony cradled the food in his palms. The warmth from them brought feeling back to his numb fingers. He scanned the alleyway. Most of the other kids had already dispersed, but a few lingered, hopeful seagulls holding out for possible scraps. The boy who'd been in front of them sat a few yards off, calmly eating. The chocolate chip muffin was gone.

"Tony?"

"Huh? Oh, yeah. They just felt good to hold for a minute."

"It'll feel even better in your stomach, mate." Miles's first muffin was gone, and he quickly started on the second.

"Yeah, you're probably right." Tony peeled the tin foil away and raised a muffin to his lips. Subtly, he sniffed, trying to detect any scents that shouldn't be there. Nothing but the spicy aroma of cinnamon flooded his senses. He parted his teeth and placed the spherical golden top against his tongue. He bit through the moist side and heaven exploded in his mouth. "Wow."

"Told ya." Miles laughed.

Tony chewed and swallowed his first bite. There was nothing suspicious— no sharp objects concealed within the cakey crust. His bites grew bolder, and before he knew it, the first muffin was gone. He had planned to ration them, but the thought of conservation was far from his mind now. He tore into the second muffin with less reserve than the first, and in moments, nothing but a crumpled wrapper remained. He cradled the last one. "Are you guys eating all of them?"

Juliette licked her fingers. "I'm saving one for later."

"Not me," Miles said, his mouth full. "I like them nice and hot. Look, I even stopped shivering." He held out his hand for them to inspect.

"Nice. I think I'll eat mine, too. Shame he doesn't serve lunch and dinner."

Miles cackled, but Juliette pursed her lips. "Just don't cry to me when you're hungry later, and if you try to filch mine, I swear I'll crack your skull while you sleep."

Miles dropped the last few crumbs into his mouth. "Whatever you say, Jules."

Juliette pocketed her last muffin, careful not to smush it against her hip, while Tony savored his last one. With each bite, he let the cake melt on his tongue and dissolve fully before swallowing.

The other kids cleared out until only their trio and the greasy haired boy remained. Tony hadn't paid attention to where the Muffin Man went, but thankfully, he was nowhere in sight. An image of the man standing there simply holding the empty muffin tray sent an unsettling breeze across the back of his neck. Miles smacked him on the upper arm and woke him from his frightening vision.

"What?"

"Come on, mate. Let's go."

"Right." Tony stood, but the huddled figure of the other boy sat crouched on the ground and made him pause. "Do you think he's okay?"

"Who?"

Tony pointed. "That kid over there. Why isn't he leaving?"

Miles shrugged and pulled his cap lower over his ears in a futile attempt to block out the cold. "Who gives a shite? Probably just wants to be first in line tomorrow."

Tony hesitated. "He looks asleep though . . . That's weird, isn't it?"

Juliette frowned. "Maybe he hadn't had food for so long that he fell asleep? I've seen that before."

Tony shook his head. "No, he told me he was here yesterday and the day before. He wasn't on the brink of starvation."

Miles lifted his ratty shirt and exposed the protruding ribs that stood out starkly against his dark flesh. "Then what do you call this, mate? We're not exactly the poster of health either."

A humorless chuckle fell from Tony's lips. "Yeah, I guess you're right."

"Let's be off, then. We can head down to the docks and see if we can pilfer some fish from the trawlers coming in."

Tony nodded and pushed the last bite of his muffin into his mouth. When he swallowed, the morsel changed to glue in his throat and creeped down— slow and laborious— until it landed in his stomach with a sour plunk. Part of him screamed not to leave the boy alone, but the other part could offer no other solution. The last thing he needed was another mouth to feed.

"Good idea," Tony agreed and plunged his hands into his pockets, shuffling after his friends.

CHAPTER 4

The next morning, the three friends were fourth in line, having woken well before dawn to secure their spot. Upon arrival, Tony searched the alleys and surrounding dumpsters, but the greasy haired boy wasn't there. His absence didn't exactly quell Tony's suspicions.

"Wow, look how many kids are already here," Juliette whispered. At least three dozen pairs of eyes glinted in the darkness.

"Word spreads fast," Miles said with a yawn. "Hopefully, the Muffin Man baked extra today."

Tony didn't reply. He was too busy scanning the growing crowd for the young boy. It may have been too dark to see clearly, but he had a sinking feeling he wouldn't find him.

"Do you know the Muffin Man, the Muffin Man, the Muffin Man? Do you know the Muffin Man, who lives on Drury Lane." Miles sang under his breath. The tune was childlike and creepy. He started again and drummed his hand on the pavement to keep time. "Do you know the Muffin—"

"What are you doing?" Tony asked. His words came out higher than he'd intended.

Miles paused and grinned. "Just trying to pass the time. Catchy, right?"

"What is it?"

Miles shrugged. "Something I made up. With word getting 'round so fast, it just sort of came to me."

"Oh. Well, could you give it a rest for a bit?"

Miles wrinkled his brow. "Sure, mate." He stopped singing but continued to quietly hum the tune to himself.

An hour later, dawn crested, and like marionettes on the ends of a puppeteer's strings, all the kids hopped to their feet and inhaled a collective breath. On cue, the Muffin Man emerged with numerous trays balanced in his hands. Amazed whispers erupted from the back, and Tony recalled experiencing the same sensation of wonder when his gaze had alighted on the fabled baker. But he didn't exclaim today. Today, he was wiser.

"Glad we got a spot upfront," Juliette spoke softly. "He only has five trays again, but there's at least double the kids there were yesterday."

"Good morning to you all. Is everybody hungry today?" The Muffin Man shouted, and calls in the affirmative echoed back. "Excellent. Today there are quite a bit more of you, but not to worry. I made a special kind of pastry. While you will only receive one, be assured that it will leave you satisfied."

"What kind are they?" a boy called from the back.

The Muffin Man cupped his hand over one ear and somehow balanced the full trays in one hand. "What was that? Are you curious what flavor the Muffin Man baked for you today?"

Tony's gut clenched as the eerie melody of Miles's song bloomed in the back of his mind. He licked his chapped lips. The baker's piercing stare found his in the crowd for one lingering moment before skipping on to another face.

The Muffin Man grinned. "Mincemeat. The last few days, I've noticed how malnourished all of you seem to be. I figured I could help start your day with some protein."

There were a few groans from the back, no doubt from the children expecting something sweet. Tony frowned. He wasn't sure what mincemeat was, but it didn't sound as if it belonged in a muffin.

The baker's eyes glazed. "You don't have to partake, children. For those who are *grateful* for a warm meal, please form a line."

The majority of them already stood in the requested formation, and even after the exhalation of disappointment, no one surrendered their spot in line. Food was food, and whoever scorned it was a fool.

The Muffin Man grinned but exposed none of his teeth. Tony shuddered at the reptilian likeness. His smile was too big, stretching impossibly wide across his face, as if he could unhinge his jaw. One by one, the children collected their breakfast. Tony waited behind Miles and Juliette today. When it was his turn, he stepped before the baker and bit the inside of his cheek.

"Was that boy from yesterday all right?" Tony asked before the man could personally greet him.

The baker cocked his head and swished his mustache. "I'm afraid I'm not sure who you mean, young man."

"Tony, what are you doing?" Miles hissed under his breath, but Tony stood firm.

"The younger boy with the hat. You gave him a special muffin yesterday. I watched you. He was right in front of me." Tony's stare hardened. He had no idea how old the baker was. He seemed timeless, as if he'd always been baking on Drury Lane and always would be.

The Muffin Man snapped his fingers and withdrew a large pastry from the tray. "Yes, that's right. The lad was tired once he put some food in his stomach. I gave him a blanket and then returned to my kitchen. When I came out to dispose of the trash, he was gone. He left my blanket, though. Is he a friend of yours?"

Tony shook his head. "No."

The baker handed Tony a dense muffin. "Well, tell him hello when you see him. Enjoy." His eyes shone blankly, and Tony was gripped with the distinct feeling that he knew more than he was letting on. He accepted his breakfast and moved to the right to join his friends. They maneuvered to the same spot they'd occupied yesterday while the Muffin Man's cheerful voice played on a loop in the background.

"Oh, whoa. That's delicious. I didn't know what to expect with that weird name and all, but it has a fruity taste to it." Miles took another large bite while Tony looked on, hesitant once more.

Encouraged by Miles's fervor, Juliette increased her nibbles to a full bite. "Wow, that *is* good. I think there's some nutmeg in here, too. The texture is a bit strange though, isn't it?" She chomped thoughtfully.

"Go on, mate," Miles said. "Before one of those sad sacks in the back makes a grab for it." He took his own advice and swallowed the last of his pastry, then licked the tips of his fingers.

Tony brought the little muffin pie to his mouth and pressed his tongue to the flaky top. He had to admit, it smelled great, but he was hung-up on the contents. Of course, he'd eaten meat before— you couldn't afford to be a vegetarian when you lived on the streets— but his gut screamed not to eat it.

Still, he took a slow bite and frowned at the texture of the thinly chopped meat as it grazed his tongue. The flavor, while sweet at first, gave way to a cloying aftertaste he couldn't identify. He swallowed, and the food slid down his throat thickly. Tony flinched. The Muffin Man stared back at him with that same unnerving grin stretched across his lips.

A frail-looking girl around his age stood before the baker, and Tony watched as the Muffin Man turned his attention to her and withdrew a muffin from inside his apron. He whispered close to her ear and patted her on the head. The girl nodded and exited the line, bringing the special treat to her lips and taking a bite. Tony's gaze slid back to the Muffin Man. The baker seemed to be waiting for Tony's attention and raised his finger to his lips, then winked before he offered the next child in line breakfast.

Tony's gut clenched and nausea gripped him. Was he the only one who had seen? Something was wrong. Terribly wrong.

Miles shook his shoulder. "Hey, you all right? You look like you've seen a ghost."

Tony spun and covered the remaining half of Juliette's muffin with his palm.

She balked. "What are you doing?"

"Stop eating."

"Why?"

Tony dropped his voice. "He put something bad in it, Jules. There's something wrong with this guy."

"What are you talking about, Tony? It's just a muffin."

"No!" Tony hissed through his teeth to keep from yelling and led his friends around the corner, out of the jolly baker's line of sight.

"Tony, what is the matter with you?"

"There was a boy yesterday. Do you remember? He was in line in front of us. The Muffin Man gave him an extra one, and after he ate it, he fell asleep. Do you see him here today? No. I think . . . I think . . . think..." A violent and sick thought entered his mind, and he threw the vile pastry to the ground. Miles and Juliette gasped in unison.

"Are you crazy?" Miles bent down to retrieve it, but Tony

slammed his foot down, smearing the flaky crust all over the bottom of his shoe.

"Tony!" Juliette admonished. "Why did you take that if you weren't going to eat it? Someone else wouldn't have had to go hungry."

"Stop! You're not listening to me," Tony said in a hoarse cry under his breath. "We need to fetch the police."

Miles scoffed. "For what?"

"I'm telling you, there is something very bad going on here."

"Because one kid didn't show up today?" Miles gestured to the large crowd behind them. "How would you even know? There are a ton of kids here today. And what are the coppers going to do about it, eh? You think they're gonna care that some orphan's gone missing?"

Juliette cocked her head. "And what proof do you have? Why can't you accept it for what it is? A kind gesture from a nice man! You don't have to be so paranoid."

Tony held up his hands. "That's not what this is. I'm telling you, the Muffin Man did something to that kid." He stabbed a finger at the destroyed muffin on the ground between them. "I'm getting the police."

Miles put his hands on Tony's shoulders and stepped toe to toe with him. "Nah, mate. I can't let you do that. Don't eat if you don't want to, but I quite like a warm breakfast that I don't have to fight for, and I'm not about to let you ruin that."

"Miles, that guy is sick. I think . . . I think he killed that kid from yesterday and—"

"And what? Sliced him up and put him in the batter?"

"Yeah."

Juliette's jaw dropped in stunned horror, but Miles wasn't fazed. He shrugged and sniffed dramatically. "Like Jules said, you ain't got no proof of that."

Tony raised himself to his full height. "Fine. You want proof?" Miles nodded and sucked his lower lip. "Come here, then." His friends followed him back around the corner, and Tony motioned for them to stay low.

"What are we supposed to be looking at?" Miles asked with disdain.

"Shh." Tony pointed to the girl he'd watched accept the special muffin. She only held one in her hand now. "The baker gave that girl the same muffin as the kid yesterday. Just watch her and you'll see."

CHAPTER 5

Fifteen minutes passed, and the trays ran dry. Like yesterday, most of the children took their breakfast and dissipated, drifting back to their usual haunts to panhandle or filch—whatever method put food in their bellies.

The Muffin Man returned inside through the rusty old door by himself. Tony kept his eye on the girl in the stained coat. He supposed it had been yellow once, but grime and constant wear had turned it a sickly hue. Like a dog with its head on a swivel, he assessed her every move and looked for signs that the drugged muffin had taken effect.

"This is stupid," Miles complained a few minutes later. "What are we supposed to see?"

"Yeah, Tony," Juliette agreed. "He's not even out here anymore."

"Just wait. I saw him give it to her." Yet the longer Tony watched, the less sure he was. She should have fallen asleep by now or at least been showing signs of drowsiness, but she continued to talk to her friend with bright eyes.

"Told ya you were being paranoid. She ate it and she's fine," Miles said.

Realization hit Tony like a hard fist, and he pushed off the brick wall.

"Tony? Where are you going?" Juliette called.

Tony wove past a dumpster and an old moldy mattress, its decayed springs coiled in flaking rust. "Just because I saw him give it to her, doesn't mean *she* ate it."

"What's he saying?" Miles asked, but Juliette didn't respond.

Tony jogged ahead and shouldered into the girls' conversation. Without greeting, he addressed the girl in the dingy coat. "Did you eat the second muffin? The small one he gave you?"

The girl frowned. "No. I offered it to a little girl who arrived late."

Dread was a lead weight in his stomach. Tony wrenched his head up and scanned the cluttered alleyway. Panicking, he whipped his attention back to the girl. "Did she leave? Where did you see her last?"

The girl's expression grew tight with concern at Tony's agitated tone. "We talked to her for a bit, and then she started yawning."

"Did she leave or lay down somewhere?"

The girl pointed to a pile of crates. "She's taking a quick nap there . . ." Her voice trailed off, and the empty space radiated a hollowness. Nearby, a metallic clang sounded. "That's weird, she was right there."

Juliette tugged on Tony's sleeve. "I think that was the Muffin Man's door."

"Oh, no." Tony raced back the way they'd come, his arms pumping at his sides, past the nasty dumpster to the green metal door. He slammed his fist against the cold surface and pounded steadily. The thunder of slapping feet echoed behind him.

"Tony, what are you doing?" Miles yelled.

"The Muffin Man took that girl just like he took the kid

yesterday. We have to stop him."

"Took who? You said he was going to take *her*." Miles gestured to the girls behind them. They had followed the fleeing trio, their eyes wide with confusion and fear.

Tony shook his head. "I was wrong. I didn't see her give the muffin away. We have to get inside." He pounded on the door again but was met with silence.

"Tony." Juliette's voice was soft but heavy with doubt.

Tony ignored her and shouted, "Hey! I know what you're doing in there. Open this door or we'll get the police."

"Christ, Tony," Miles seethed through clenched teeth. "Just leave it alone. There's nothing going on here. If you bring the cops, they'll make him shut the whole thing down."

"Good. He's killing kids, Miles, and feeding us to each other. Don't you get it?" Tony banged the door once more, and this time, the latch gave way and swung open to reveal a narrow breadth of black space within. Terror and hope surged in his chest as he looked over his shoulder at the gathered group. "Get the police and make sure they check inside. I'm going in to find her or any evidence I can."

"Tony, no!" Juliette grabbed his hand.

The girls blanched and stepped back, and Miles shook his head. "I'm not going in there, mate."

Tony fixed him with a hard stare. "I'm not asking you to. Just get the cops." He turned and shook out of Juliette's hold, inhaled a shaky breath, and slipped inside.

CHAPTER 6

His name ricocheted off the walls as he plunged deeper into the darkness. He was touched by the desperation in his friends' cries, but nothing could deter him from his mission. He knew the baker was up to something, and he refused to let it go until he proved it. Tony prayed they listened and found the police. He wasn't stupid. He was no match for a psychotic killer and didn't stand a chance getting back out, but he couldn't stand by while innocent kids were murdered. Life was hard enough without being preyed upon.

Tony moved through the dimly lit hall, surprised no foul odors or garbage lingered. In fact, the twisting labyrinth was pristine. Up ahead, the corridor curved to the left and brightened. Several candles burned low and offered enough light for him to continue. He was in a storeroom. Each shelf was lined and organized with precision, every item an equal distance from its neighbor.

He scanned the ingredients. Bags of flour, jars of semisweet chocolate chips, and pallets of sugar met his gaze. Spices loomed above. Cinnamon, rosemary, clove, ginger, and nutmeg were the few he recognized, among others whose labels Tony had never heard of.

A rounded archway was tucked off to the left. The first room had yielded nothing suspicious or out of the ordinary, but perhaps the baker kept another pantry where the more sinister ingredients were stored. Tony calculated every slow step lest he trip and alert the Muffin Man to his presence. The dark hallway meandered farther into the building's stomach. Strange there were no other offshoots or doorways. He shivered at the thought of the corridor collapsing and burying him inside. He swallowed the intrusive image and kept going.

At last, an obstruction blocked his path. Four thick plastic panels hung like bleached bones across the threshold to another room. The antechamber was illuminated, but the large panels made it impossible to see what awaited on the other side.

He stepped as close to the gently swaying panels as he could without making contact and peered through the narrow gap. A steel table— waist high— stood in the middle of the space, a pile of dirty rags its only occupant. It wasn't until Tony caught sight of a cleaned forearm that he realized it was a person. The little girl. She wasn't moving. Hopefully, it was a side effect of whatever mixture the Muffin Man had drugged the food with rather than a permanent state he'd already rendered.

Tony's heart raced, and he pushed his face forward. The cold plastic grazed his cheeks, and goose bumps rippled down his neck. From what he could see, the rest of the room was empty. If he was quick, he could grab the girl and rush out the back door before the baker returned. He licked his lips and flexed his hands, readying himself for the necessary burst of energy.

Tony pushed the middle panel to the side to allow enough room for his thin frame to sneak through, but movement materialized to his right. He pressed his lips into a narrow line to contain his yelp of surprise as the Muffin Man emerged from the corner of the room with a large bucket in one hand and a gleaming silver carving knife in the other. The plastic panels fluttered in response to Tony's sharp flinch and clacked together until they settled into place.

His throat swelled as the baker glanced over and fixed his eerie eyes on the spot Tony had just occupied. Tony slunk farther back into the shadows and shut his eyes, willing himself to disappear. Five tense heartbeats passed, and the baker continued to the table and his silent guest.

Tony opened his eyes and tiptoed back toward the panels. If only his adversary would leave the room again. He needed thirty seconds. Thirty seconds and he and the girl could escape and disappear in London's smog and puddle-strewn streets. He'd never liked the rain and had spent many damp nights cursing the clouds for their endless sobs, but right now, standing in the dank hallway surrounded by the metallic stench of serrated steel and fear, he'd give anything to be outside breathing the earthy fresh scent of the rain.

Over Tony's thundering heart, the Muffin Man hummed a cheery tune that clashed with the nightmarish scene. He dragged the girl to the edge of the table and positioned her head so that it was hanging off the lip of the surface. He snapped his fingers and his head jerked up as if he'd forgotten something. The happy song grew louder as he marched to the left and out of sight.

Tony strained his ears until the baker's music was inaudible. Swallowing his terror, he pushed through the panels. This was his only chance to save her. He scanned the direction the Muffin Man had exited and spied a swinging door nestled between two large wooden barrels. Sacks of flour and sugar slouched at the base, and a hook of aprons hung on the wall to the right.

With the coast as clear as it was going to get, Tony raced to the table and slid his hands beneath the girl's still form. She was clammy, but he garnered strength from the fact that she was still breathing. They could both make it out alive.

Tony shifted the child's weight onto his forearms and took a step back when a sharp bite, like the slice of a rat's incisors, caught him by surprise. He tossed his head and shrieked. The Muffin Man was crouched behind him, his cold eyes like glass as he stared back. In his hand, an empty syringe winked, and the tip of the needle glistened with a scarlet sheen.

CHAPTER 7

A dozen thoughts flickered through Tony's mind, specifically the instinct to flee, but before he could form a solid plan, his brain fogged and his limbs grew sluggish. The girl turned to lead in his arms, and he collapsed against the table, spilling her back onto the hard surface. At the same time, his knees gave out below the injection site, and he crashed to the floor in a crumpled heap.

Behind him, the baker stood and set the syringe on top of one of the barrels. "Smarts a bit, doesn't it?" he asked in his breathy high-pitched voice. "This concoction is derived from the pufferfish. Do you know what that is? See, unlike Rose here who ingested opium, you will stay awake and feel . . . *everything*." The Muffin Man giggled like a conspiring toddler. "I mean, why shouldn't you? You're the first to sneak into my home. The first to suspect. Seems only fair to reward your tenacity with the truth of my little operation."

The baker wrapped Tony in a bear hug and lugged his paralyzed body toward the wall, keeping him in sight of the table and the unmoving body atop it. Obscenities screamed in Tony's mind, but his tongue sat uselessly in his mouth like a dead slug.

"I must admit, you caught on rather quickly. Much faster than the last lad in Paris. I reckon it's my eyes, huh? They're a bit unnerving. Well, no matter. Now comes the fun part, and lucky you, you have a front row seat."

Tony's eyes slid to the right as he slouched. He had the same amount of control over his body as a boat tossed about in a storm. The Muffin Man untied his loose apron and pulled the strings taut once more before retying them. He picked up the blade and stood at the head of the table, his feet planted on either side of the bucket. No new instruments had graced the scene since his last departure, and Tony realized he'd played right into the baker's trap. He'd known Tony was standing just outside and had created an opportunity for Tony to willingly enter the hellish chamber of his own accord.

The Muffin Man tilted Rose's head back to expose the smooth column of her neck. Too late did Tony understand the baker's intent. A gurgling sounded in Tony's throat as he tried to scream. He tried to shut his eyes, but the paralysis refused him even a moment's reprieve from the horror.

Angling the blade at a forty-five-degree slant, the Muffin Man sliced through Rose's throat nearly ear to ear. The squelching sound of tearing flesh caused Tony's stomach to clench, threatening to vomit. A chorus of bubbling resounded, accompanied by a wet slap as torrents of blood streamed into the tin bucket below. Unable to move or escape the sight, Tony was forced to watch as the ruby blood ran faster. The hollow plinking quickly extinguished as the bottom of the pail became saturated. Rose's pale complexion turned white as bone as the last of her blood drained.

The Muffin Man set the knife down with a clatter atop the metal surface and looked at Tony over his shoulder. "The mince meat pies were such a hit. I planned on making them— plus blueberry— tomorrow, but with all this meat, I'll have enough for bourekas too."

Tony leaned against the bottom shelf, compelled to remain silent.

"Bourekas. Flaky pastries filled with ground beef, onions, and pine nuts. A delicious way to start the day." The baker waltzed to the large barrel on the left and opened the lid. Grayed fingertips poked out of its depths. Inside, Tony screamed as he pictured the greasy haired boy. How many pieces of him remained?

"You see, for the majority to live, a few must die. I'm not one to play favorites. I only offer death to those I can tell are struggling harder than most. I offer a peaceful end, don't you see? I erase their suffering so others can grow strong. That's why I started doing this. No one else seems to care about the poor orphans or runaways filling the city, but I do." He pointed to his chest, hard enough to leave a bruise. "I care. I love transforming despair into hope. To give a child on the verge of death one more day. By sacrificing one, I save dozens. Wouldn't you do the same?"

Tony managed to grit his teeth, but the venomous insults he wished to hurl at the deranged baker sat lodged in his throat. He thought himself a hero.

The Muffin Man withdrew a different blade from the well of his apron and stood to the side. He stretched Rose's arm above her head and with a practiced swing, brought the knife down to the right of her shoulder. There wasn't much meat clinging to her petite frame, so the blade cut through the muscle easily. Only a slight amount of pressure was necessary to snap the humerus, and in under a minute, her left arm had been severed. He placed it in the barrel and poured salt, not flour like Tony originally thought, from the burlap sack and replaced the lid.

Tony's stomach lurched again. He knew salt preserved meat. His eyes took stock of all the barrels. It was impossible to know for certain how many children he'd killed and served each day. He couldn't even guess how old the baker was. His face had a timelessness that appeared both young and ancient, like an optical illusion.

The Muffin Man took his place at the steel table once more and made short work of the rest of Rose's limbs. Her right femur put up quite a fight, but with a bit more pressure, the baker was able to cut through it.

Tony had no way of knowing how long the effects of the poison the Muffin Man injected him with would last. He focused all his energy on moving his fingers. One step at a time. A heavy 'thunk' echoed as the baker added the rest of Rose's limbs to the barrel while Tony managed to shift his focus to the faraway wall rather than at the increasing horror of the grisly scene. One small victory.

CHAPTER 8

"Shepherd's pie would be lovely as well," The Muffin Man spoke to himself. "Served alongside a delicious biscuit." He sighed contently. "You're going to feed so many children. You can take comfort in that."

Tony wished to scream and smash all the neatly ordered jars onto the concrete floor, but the drug continued to wield a comatose spell. Only the slightest puff of air signaled his rage.

The Muffin Man picked up the crimson stained blade and sliced through the large gash on Rose's throat. Void of all tethers, Rose's head spun backward and bounced onto the floor with a wet smack. The momentum wasn't enough to send it rolling. Instead, the slick tissue stuck to the concrete at an odd angle. Rose's face turned toward Tony. He was grateful her eyelids stayed closed.

"I don't think you children understand just how much work goes into providing for you." The baker twisted the remaining torso in front of him and stood it up before stripping it of the grimy clothing. He threw the rags into a square hole in the wall across from Tony and then pressed a button beside it.

Red and orange embers illuminated as the incinerator thrummed to life. What little hope Tony harbored that the police would come evaporated. Even if they did investigate his friends' claim, the only evidence they'd discover would be barrels of salt and piles of charred ash. His will crumbled. Once he was through with Rose, the Muffin Man would start preparing him.

"The moment I finish serving breakfast, I return to my kitchen and clean up my workspace. I sanitize the tables and instruments while I wait for the chosen child to succumb to the heavy sleep. Once they've fallen under, I bring them back here and begin butchering new meat for the next day's meal. The entire process takes hours. I'm up well into the night, and then I wake at five to start baking so the food is hot and fresh for you at sunrise."

The Muffin Man fished a filet knife from the depths of his apron and pinched the tiniest bit of fat on Rose's hips between his fingers, then edged the tip of the blade through. The sound of serrated steel tearing flesh interrupted the quiet as he flayed her skin with precise cuts. Tony tried to touch his fingertips together, yet his body still refused to comply.

He watched while the baker peeled large flaps of skin back to reveal pink tissue beneath. The smell was ungodly—something forbidden and internal. The Muffin Man exchanged knife after knife, each one more adept at carving what little meat Rose possessed from her ribs. He sorted the pieces into multiple piles, but by what category, Tony couldn't discern.

Numerous pockets of blood popped within Rose's body as he dissected deeper. Thin red rivulets spilled over the beveled edge of the table and ran freely to the floor. Tony looked into the baker's eyes and doubted he even realized the mess he'd created. He was a man possessed, lost in the rhythmic sawing of the blade and glossy surface of each organ as he pried them loose from their cavities and stroked their smooth surfaces.

There was no longer any way to identify Rose. He had reduced her to five glistening slabs of meat. Apart from her decapitated head sitting three feet from Tony's shoe, he would have assumed he was in an ordinary butcher's shop, but there was nothing ordinary about this man.

"Poor thing didn't have much to give, did she? But beggars can't be choosers." The Muffin Man waggled his eyebrows at Tony and smiled his large grin again, the eeriness heightened by the dark blood coating his arms up to his elbows. "Lucky for your friends that you showed up. Otherwise, breakfast would have been pretty light tomorrow. Everything always seems to work itself out."

Tony rumbled low in the back of his throat. He wished he could express his objections more soundly, rather than with his pathetic utterance, but the drug was too slow to filter out of his system.

Like a switch being thrown, the Muffin Man's eyes lost the crazed sheen and adopted a meticulous manner instead. In minutes, he had carried away the parts of Rose he would use in his pastries tomorrow on a silver cookie sheet and mopped up the congealing blood growing thick on the floor.

Tony exhaled, the sound like a deflating balloon. His time in the baker's dimly lit basement was coming to an end. He tried to find the will to fight, to scrounge up the courage for one last attempt to escape his fate, but he was so tired. He had fought every day since his mother left him at the age of six. Fought for food, clean water, warmth, and a place to sleep. Otherwise, the streets would have swallowed him up. His body would have been just another load for the garbage men to haul away. He supposed there *was* something poetic about the Muffin Man's vision. If one of them wasn't going to survive, it made sense that their body be used to nourish those who would.

Tony pictured Miles and Juliette. Would they put it all together? He hoped they would stay away from Drury Lane. They were clever and resilient. They didn't need the baker's handouts. His eyes grew heavy and began to mist over. The room dissolved into a kaleidoscope of blurred colors and shadows— red being the most prominent. He hoped if any of the other kids caught on to the Muffin Man's scheme, they would be smarter than he was and find a way to stop him once and for all.

The baker clapped his hands. The table's silver surface glistened once again. "All right, looks like it's your turn. Good thing, too. That poison should be wearing off." He bent down and cradled Tony in his arms, much like a loving father might carry his son. But there was no love in the baker's eyes, only glee as he led his calf to slaughter.

He laid Tony on the cool slab and positioned his body in the same manner as Rose's. As the baker dragged him to the edge and pulled the crown of his head over, Tony found he could move his hand. His fingers twitched, then balled into a tight fist. The toxin was molten fire as it drained from his veins. Just a few more minutes and he might be strong enough to roll off the table and dive through the plastic panels.

Tony raised his forearm an inch off the table. Tingling shocks prickled up and down his limbs as feeling returned. Hope surged as the metallic clang of a fresh bucket clattered beneath his head. The Muffin Man stood above, but the wicked gleam of the butcher knife dominated his vision. His stomach flipped when the baker smiled, but from his perspective, the grin was a giant frown.

This time, the baker showed his teeth. A frowning skeleton. The blade kissed the column of Tony's throat. Another garbled breath fell from his lips as he concentrated all his energy into his fist. He kept his eyes locked on the Muffin Man and aimed the punch at his sagging mouth. Out of the corner of his eye, he watched his fist advance. He was so close. He imagined the satisfying sound of enamel cracking, and his lips quirked with frozen laughter.

Rather than the crunch he expected, the ring of steel crescendoed instead. For a moment, all thoughts suspended. Then the pain attacked, as if he'd grabbed a skillet off a hot stove and forgotten how to let go. Tony tried to shake his hand and relieve the sensation, but it only intensified.

His eyes rolled, and a shower of warm red pepper flakes sprinkled his face, followed by a pool of wetness that soaked into his shirt. The blade in the Muffin Man's hand was now laced with webs of crimson. An object landed with a dull thud on Tony's chest.

Tony stared at his mutilated forearm that he had wielded with so much hope just seconds ago. With one fell swoop of his knife, the Muffin Man had eliminated his last chance of escape. Always one step ahead.

"That was a noble effort, young man, but enough games, eh?"

Without another word, the Muffin Man sliced the knife across Tony's throat, deep enough to glimpse the wink of white bone beneath. A thin red line dribbled out of the corner of his mouth as his vision blurred. Death was not grand and swooped in fast and unyielding.

"That's better," the baker said as Tony's eyes glazed with death. He brandished the thick butcher knife and set to work ridding Tony of his clothes with skillful cuts. The cheerful tune he'd heard the children singing earlier filled the kitchen. "Do you know the Muffin Man, the Muffin Man, the Muffin Man. Do you know the Muffin Man who kills on Drury Lane?"

The End

"Hickory Dickory Dock" is a beloved nursery rhyme that has delighted children for centuries and is a fun way to help them learn to count as the clock continues to chime. The rhyme is likely based on the Exeter Cathedral in Exeter, England. Home to the Exeter Cathedral astronomical clock, made in the 1400s, it is seen as an intricate and beautiful invention with a fun twist.

As a devout cat lover, I was tickled to learn that this clock includes a special hole for the cathedral guard cat to use to keep the grand timepiece free of mice.

In my story, I do not have a cat, but there is a guard of a more sinister nature. Playing off the stressors of a new move, sibling rivalry, and the assumption that young children tend to fabricate outlandish tales, this small family is in for a frightening night of horrors as the grandfather clock's chimes echo through the isolating darkness.

Enjoy.

Uitti, Jacob. (2023, April). *Behind the Classic Perseverant Nursery Rhyme "Hickory Dickory Dock."* American Songwriter. http://americansongwriter.com

CAYTLYN BROOKE

INFERNAL CHIMES

CHAPTER 1

"Mom, Lena hit me!" Maddie shouted from the back seat.

"Only because you've been poking me for the last hour." Lena adjusted her earbuds and crossed her arms.

"That doesn't mean you can hit me!"

Lena yanked the toy elephant out of Maddie's hands and held it out the window. Maddie screeched, reaching a decibel that threatened to shatter the windshield.

"Give Ellie back!" Maddie arched in her seat, and her skinny arms careened as if she were about to take flight.

"Promise to stop touching me," Lena said.

"Mom!"

"Lena, so help me, if you don't bring that elephant back into the car this second, I will throw your phone in the river!" Their mother's knuckles grew into stark ridges over the steering wheel. She didn't turn around to confront Lena, but she didn't have to. Her exhaustion and frayed nerves had been evident since Omaha. As they pushed through the final leg of their journey, the large gas station coffee she'd ordered was long gone and her mental state had reverted back to a precarious position of fragility.

Lena rolled her eyes. "Okay, geez. It was just a joke." She pulled the imperiled pachyderm out of the wind. Without looking at Maddie, Lena tossed the toy at her and glared at the headrest.

"Ha ha," their mother said without humor. "We're all very entertained." Her eyes shifted from the rearview mirror to the left side of the vehicle. "Maddie, stop screaming or you're going to make me drive off the road."

"Okay, Mama." Maddie wiped the tears from her reddened eyes.

"We talked about this, remember? A new life, a new start. And look at us. We're not even to Wyoming yet, and we've fallen right back into the same habits." She exhaled a long breath. "I don't want to yell anymore, okay? So, can we please try to get along and treat each other nicely?"

"Yes," Maddie whispered as she cradled Ellie.

"Yes." Lena's acknowledgment was even more lackluster.

"Thank you." An uncomfortable silence enveloped the small car. Their mother sighed again and pointed to a passing road sign. "Look, Casper in eight miles. We're almost there."

"Good, because this car smells like ass."

"Mom, Lena said a bad word."

The tires squealed in protest as the treads bumped over the rumble strip and onto the shoulder. Mom slammed her palms against the steering wheel. "Enough! I don't want to hear another word from either of you. I am done. I don't care that you hate each other. I don't care that you hate me for moving you across the country. I don't care that you think Dad is the fun parent. We're stuck together, whether you like it or not." The anger deflated and left her voice brittle and small. "This is really hard for me to leave everything behind— but I'm trying to make the best of a bad situation. I just need a little help."

Maddie leaned forward and placed a gentle hand on her mom's shoulder. "I'm sorry."

"Me too," Lena agreed. This time, her apology was hoarse with sincerity.

Mom reached up and clasped Maddie's tiny hand. "Thank you."

Maddie drew back and gave Lena a small smile, signaling a temporary truce. The car bumped along the uneven shoulder as Mom pulled back out onto the empty highway. The uneasy tension lightened with every mile marker they passed, and the atmosphere was amicable for the first time since they'd left New York.

"We're going to have a great new life here. I can feel it."

"Do they have a gymnastics team?" Maddie asked hopefully.

Her mom smiled in the rearview mirror. "I'm not sure, baby, but I'll ask around. And Lena, we'll see if there's an art studio nearby where you can continue your lessons." The forced cheerfulness in her tone was hard to miss.

"Sounds cool," Lena replied.

A few minutes later, the car veered off into the exit lane and rolled through a stop sign to continue to the right. "Okay," Mom said as she peered over the steering wheel into the expansive darkness. "The road should be up here on the left. Everyone keep your eyes out."

"How can we see with our eyes out of our heads?" Maddie asked and crinkled her nose.

"It's just an expression that means to look, honey."

"Oh." Maddie pressed her little face to her window, but the sedan's headlights didn't illuminate past the passenger side door. Thick plains cottonwood trees stood sentry along the road's edge, silent giants shielding buried secrets from curious onlookers. Frail brown leaves littered the forest floor as their headlights swept over them. Maddie shivered. How many years of decaying leaves would need to fall to cover a dead body?

Maddie shook her head and squeezed her elephant tighter. She was scaring herself unnecessarily, but she couldn't help it. The woods were a mystery to her. All of her third-grade teachers had noted her wild imagination, but she didn't understand why they scowled every time they mentioned it. Indulging in imagination kept her on her toes and allowed her to see the world through a different lens than the narrow scope her fifteen-year-old sister never looked away from. She peered harder into the trees and spied a small hunched figure shrouded in shadow a few feet back from the road.

"Mom, stop."

"What?" Shrieking brakes accompanied her mother's frantic voice.

"I think I just saw a little boy."

"A boy? Out here?"

Lena put down her phone and scanned the dark trees where Maddie pointed. "Where was he?"

"Over there, back a little bit."

Mom shifted the car into reverse and backed up.

"There!"

The car rocked as Mom stepped on the brake, no doubt terrified that the solid thud of flesh hitting metal would follow, but nothing but the hoot of an owl sounded in the dark night as they stared into the tree line. Lena unbuckled her seat belt and climbed over to Maddie's side.

"Can you see him, Lena?" Mom asked.

Lena didn't reply. Maddie's heart raced, and she took comfort in her sister's weight against her. After a few seemingly endless seconds, Lena exhaled a deep breath and pushed off the window. "It's only a mailbox, ding-dong."

"What?"

"Are you sure?" Mom asked.

Lena scoffed and resumed scrolling on her phone. "Yeah, it's all mangled, like someone hit it. That's why it's all lopsided."

Maddie pressed her nose against the glass. She was sure it had been a boy, yet as the car drove closer and the headlights flooded the scene, she realized her sister was right. Hanging upside down on a cracked wooden post was a black box, the kind large enough to fit a small dog.

"Mom, what are you doing?" Lena asked as they deviated from the main road.

"What does that say? Eleven?" Mom squinted, leaning over the dashboard.

"It looks like two claw marks," Maddie volunteered.

"Great. This is us," Mom said. She jerked the wheel and turned onto the leaf-strewn driveway.

"You've got to be kidding. Is the rest of the house falling apart, too?"

"No, Lena. Like you said, someone probably hit the mailbox. I can go to the hardware store tomorrow."

They drove down the lane, but Maddie twisted around and glanced back at the mailbox. She shivered and chewed the inside of her cheek. The box's mouth had fallen open, and the black maw gaped wide, belching even more darkness into the night.

CHAPTER 2

The front door wouldn't open. Maddie's mom fit the key into the lock and jiggled the handle, but the rusted hinges held firm in their resolve to keep them out. Maddie snuggled her stuffed elephant. It seemed as if the house were preventing them from entering on purpose.

Mom threw up her hands in defeat. "Fine. We'll have to find a motel to spend the night, and I can call a locksmith first thing in the morning." She raised her phone and tapped the screen, then dug the heels of her palms into her eyes and groaned. "No service? I don't need this right now."

Maddie stood silently and waited. It was best to make herself invisible whenever Mom was stressed. No matter what Maddie said, it always seemed to trigger her, and she didn't want to be scolded, especially standing out there in the chilly darkness.

"Move over," Lena said and hipped Mom out of the way.

"Lena, it won't budge."

Lena let her backpack drop to the dilapidated brick entryway and stomped toward the door. With a quick inhale, she gripped the doorframe with both hands and delivered a hard swift kick to the space just below the keyhole. Unable to withstand the brutal onslaught, the wood splintered and gave way. The door swung inward, and the lock hung askew, dangling like a loose tooth.

Lena sniffed against the cold and pivoted on her worn Converse. She scooped her backpack off the ground with one hand and hoisted it up to rest between her shoulder blades.

"Was that necessary?" Mom asked.

Lena crossed the porch again and nudged the door open the rest of the way with her foot. "It beats sleeping in the car or wandering aimlessly until we find some sleazy motel that you'll whine about having to pay for. We can prop a chair under the handle or something so no one can get in. It'll be fine." She strode into the darkness and activated her phone's flashlight. "There's no one out here, anyway."

"A chair? We don't have any furniture, Lena. And I really don't care for your snotty attitude." Mom yanked the key from the lock before pocketing it.

"Don't think you need to worry about that first bit," Lena answered from inside the cavernous home. Her voice was flat and sent chills down Maddie's spine.

"What are you talking about? Come on, Maddie." Mom ushered Maddie inside and dragged her My Little Pony suitcase behind them. They crossed the threshold, then froze. "Oh my."

From within Lena's spotlight, fully furnished rooms greeted them. Well-worn couches, adorned coffee tables, and dust-covered oriental rugs decorated every surface. But the furniture wasn't draped in white sheets like Maddie had seen in movies. Side tables lay overturned, lamps were shattered, and old dishes had been placed around the coffee table like a haunted tea party. The uncomfortable feeling that had prickled Maddie outside increased tenfold into a physical weight she couldn't pry from her chest.

Lena shined her flashlight back and forth. "This isn't creepy at all."

"Maybe there was an emergency and the last family had to

leave suddenly?" Mom guessed.

Lena slowly spun, suspicion scowled across her face— an expression her severe black eyeliner only enhanced. "I thought Grandma gave you the key. Whose house was this?"

Mom bit her lip. "Ah, Uncle Tommy's."

"Uncle Tommy?" Lena's mouth gaped and her eyes bulged. "The one in the nut house?"

"Hospital," Mom corrected. "And yes."

"But—"

"Lena."

"I'm not staying here."

Maddie looked up from the cobwebbed and crumb-laden plates.

Mom pinned Lena with an icy look that made Maddie shrink even though she wasn't the recipient. "Where else do you suggest we go? Huh? Your father left us with nothing. This is the best I can do until I find a steady job."

Lena set her lips in a thin line and crossed her arms in silent surrender.

"What happened here?" Maddie asked. "Who's Uncle Tommy?"

Mom shot Lena a dark look and moved to where Maddie stood at the entrance to the living room and crouched down. "Uncle Tommy is my brother. He used to live here. There's nothing wrong with this house, sweetheart. It just needs some work."

Maddie's large brown eyes shifted to Lena's aggressive posture. "Then why is Lena mad?"

Her mom's eyes flickered back and forth, but Lena spoke before she could answer.

"I'm always mad, Maddie Cake. But Mom's right. The house is fine. Want to go pick out our room?"

Maddie grinned. "Yeah."

"Come on." Lena held out her hand.

A surge of excitement welled in Maddie's tiny frame. Lena was never nice to her. She fit her hand into her sister's and admired the chipped midnight-black nail polish on Lena's chewed fingernails. Maddie dreamed of the day Mom would allow her to paint her nails, too. Together they climbed the carpeted stairs until her sneakers balanced on the top step.

Dong. Dong. Dong.

A guttural chime bellowed through the home. Maddie screamed and buried her face in Lena's stomach.

"What the hell is that?" Lena yelled.

Mom threw her arm in the direction of a hulking figure poised in the hallway that led away from the front door. "A grandfather clock. They sound every hour."

Maddie could hardly hear over the deep gong and squeezed her eyes shut, praying it would end. After ten strikes, it quieted at last, and the final ring echoed like a canon blast in her ear drums. Silence radiated. Everyone was too nervous to speak lest the clock start up again.

Lena sighed. "That was obnoxious."

Maddie lowered her hands and peered past the ornate banister to the towering clock's silhouette. It stood cloaked in inky pools of shadow that seemed to drip in curtains of thick sludge.

"I'll try to disconnect that first thing tomorrow," Mom said. "Though, I might have to call someone. Those old clocks are like your grandpa. Tough and don't like to quit."

"We have to listen to that all night?" Maddie asked.

"You can wear your headphones and listen to music, honey."

Lena rolled her eyes. "Come on, Mads. Let's go find a room."

CHAPTER 3

Lena flicked the light switch and illuminated a small office. Bookshelves lined the walls, and a large wooden desk sat in the back left corner. The chair drooped in an expression of fatigue, and a single exposed bulb threw yellowed light around the walls, highlighting at least a dozen dirty mirrors, all aimed at the door.

Maddie slunk around her sister. Multiple versions of herself were reflected back at her. Why had all these mirrors been collected and staged in here? She scanned the rest of the room. Papers with scrawled writing littered the desk's surface, and an overturned cup of coffee left their messages grainy and wrinkled.

Maddie ran her finger along the wooden edge of a tall mirror. Dust coated her skin. This room possessed the same chaotic energy as the living room.

"No beds," Lena declared. "Let's try the other room."

Maddie pivoted on her heels and followed Lena to the other end of the hall. The pale wooden door was open and offered a narrow glimpse into the opaque bedroom beyond.

"Can you go first?" Maddie asked in a small voice.

"Sure." Her sister snaked her arm into the doorway and felt for the light switch while keeping the rest of her body in the hall. Maddie held her breath. Lena's arm looked like a stump in her black sweater, amputated at the shoulder. Her sister was fine, but the illusion terrified Maddie.

Lena gave a victorious sigh, and a faint click resounded. The same sallow yellow light from the office flooded the room. Lena pushed the door open the rest of the way, and her shoulders sagged. "Great. One bed. At least it looks big enough for both of us."

Maddie ran over and flopped down on the pale pink quilt. "Ew, it's so dusty." A sneeze tickled her nose. "How are we going to sleep on this?"

"Let me have it. Jump off."

Lena grabbed the edge of the coverlet, and once Maddie's feet hit the floor, she yanked it off the bed. The faded material puddled at her feet. She gathered it in her arms, and her lips pursed in a disgusted expression as she exited the room.

The floorboards creaked as Lena moved back into the office, and a repetition of heavy thuds followed as she beat the dust off the quilt with what Maddie assumed were hearty slaps of her hands. Maddie walked the perimeter of her new bedroom and left grimy streaks atop the dresser and the dozen or so knickknacks that stared at her through fine layers of dust.

An uneasy feeling settled on Maddie's shoulders, as if she were no longer the only one in the room, but she shook it off and brushed grime from a small silver disc the size of her palm and clicked its delicate clasp. The top flipped open, revealing two circular mirrors. She traced the beautiful edge. It felt almost wet to the touch, and the dust clung to her finger in a fuzzy cap. A long black shadow flickered in the spotted glass's reflection over her shoulder. Maddie yelped.

She spun around and clutched Ellie to her chest. "Lena?" The laborious thumps from down the hall continued. Her sister wasn't pranking her. "Hello?"

A cold breeze ruffled the ends of her mousy brown hair, but the only window was closed and looked like it hadn't been opened in years. Unease prickled along the back of Maddie's neck and caused her skin to flush. Her eyes roamed the frozen figurines on the dresser, frightened she might catch one of them mid-blink. Swallowing the growing lump in her throat, she took a step closer to them.

As she shuffled forward, her foot came to rest on a fluffy object that squished beneath her sock. Her shrill scream rent the air when she spied a pair of beady black eyes staring at her from beneath her big toe. The bedroom erupted into bedlam as Maddie leapt onto the bed at the same time Mom and Lena raced through the door, bumbling against one another to reach her first.

"What is it?" Mom asked.

"Why are you screaming?" Lena yelled.

Maddie closed her mouth, seeming to draw all sound from the room. "There was a mouse."

Lena groaned. "A mouse? Seriously? You used to have a gerbil."

"Hamster," Maddie corrected. "And I stepped on it. It felt all rubbery under my foot."

Mom extended her arms, and Maddie fell into them with relief. She buried her nose in the exposed skin of her collarbone, but the spicy floral scent she sought was nowhere to be found. Mom used to smell like that all the time— her favorite perfume— until she learned Dad had gifted his girlfriend the same bottle. Now, she only smelled of the Dove soap she showered with.

Lena dumped the quilt on the edge of the bed and dropped to her hands and knees, scanning the floor for the fluffy culprit.

"Well, it's gone now. You scared it away. Are you sure it wasn't your stuffed animal?"

Maddie narrowed her eyes. "I was holding Ellie the whole time."

Mom sighed. "It's an old house. There's bound to be a few mice." She patted Maddie's knee. "Come on. Let's brush our teeth and put on some pajamas. We can unpack tomorrow."

Mom scooped Maddie off the bed and deposited her back onto the worn area rug. It was a terrible color. Maroon splotches covered the dingy gray fibers.

"Thanks for shaking off the blanket, Lena." Mom gave her a light squeeze around her upper arm. "I brought the bag with your toothbrushes in from the car. There's only one bathroom downstairs by my room. Let's get ready for bed, and then I'll tuck you in."

Maddie and Lena butted elbows as they fought over the sink while trying to outdo one another with the largest glob of spit.

Maddie spat another turquoise bubble into the basin and flashed her teeth toward the little mirror she'd found upstairs. Like the rest of the house, the one that had hung above the vanity had been torn down and was probably among the collection that littered the office floor. As she scrubbed her molars, she studied the dark green shower curtain printed with white flowers. It took her a minute to realize it was mold.

In the mirror, the shadow from before flickered and turned its head before it ducked behind the clear liner. Maddie whipped around, and her toothbrush clattered into the bowl, spraying Lena's hand with frothy spit.

"Gross! What's your deal?"

Maddie didn't answer. The strange shadow fled, taking with it the same sensation of being watched she'd felt upstairs. Her foot slid over the brown plush mat before the tub, and her fingers gripped the plastic edge of the moldy curtain. Her heart raced. What would she find inside? A ghost? A creepy face? Before she could talk herself out of it, she tore back the curtain and smacked the discolored liner out of the way. The tub was empty save for the rust-colored stains that marred the porcelain.

Lena shoved her shoulder. "Hello? You can't just throw your spit all over me."

"There was something here. It was watching us." Maddie let the curtain fall, but her eyes didn't leave the spot.

"Cut it out, Mads. I'm tired."

"I swear. I saw a shadow."

Lena rolled her eyes. "Yeah, yours, dumbo. Look." She waved her arm, and the space behind her darkened as her shadow cast on the sharp corner of the intersecting walls. "Wipe that up and get upstairs so Mom can tuck you in. I'm so done with this day."

Lena pushed past her into the dimly lit hall. Shivers tickled the back of Maddie's neck as the feeling of being watched returned. She didn't bother telling Lena she was wrong. Her sister would have only made fun of her, but the shadows weren't the same. Only hers painted the wall now, but that didn't erase the unease that curled like a tight turtleneck against her throat.

Maddie pushed the shower curtain all the way to the side while the rusted rings shrieked against the metal rod. Now, her imagination wouldn't have a chance to invent creepy beings. She twisted the tap, washed the toothpaste off her brush, and swished a handful of water in her mouth before spitting it down the silver drain. Mom hadn't unpacked any of their cups yet, so she tossed her toothbrush on the counter beside Lena's and walked out. Lena could deny it all she wanted, but there was something in the house with them.

CHAPTER 4

Lena's soft snores whispered along with the upbeat tempo that poured from her earbuds. The lyrics were hard to make out, even while Maddie lay beside her. She envied her sister's ability to shut out the world. Maddie had lain awake for hours already. She'd always been a light sleeper, but something had roused her between her dreams and forced her to pay attention. A dark ocean of shapes loomed in the blackness of the room, seeming to move and shift as her eyes dilated. The cherry-red numbers of Lena's alarm clock resembled a pair of eyes: 2:58 a.m. Far too early to turn on the light and read. Maddie could hear her sister's insults already.

At the scurrying of tiny clawed feet along the top of her dresser, Maddie pushed off the covers and balanced on her knees while her heart hammered. With help from a bare bulb that shone through the window from over the one-bay garage, she was just able to make out the dust-covered objects she'd observed earlier. Edging closer, she found the source of the sound.

Sitting on its hind legs, a mouse rubbed its front paws over its face, indulging in a quick bath. Her fearful imaginings fled. "Hello again," she whispered. "I'm glad to see you're not hurt." The mouse didn't pause its bathing and closed its eyes as it ruffled the fur on its head. She squinted harder. Was it a trick of the light or was it bald in places? "Can I ask you a question? Is there something bad in this house?"

Glassy black eyes shot open at the same time its little mouth parted. A thunderous bellow roared from its dark throat and sent a ripple of bone-rattling vibrations through Maddie's frame. The mouse's eyes held her hostage, electrifying her to the spot. Its stare was far too heavy for a rodent. Then, a metallic peal echoed through the house. It wasn't until it chimed for the third time and then grew silent that Maddie realized it was the old grandfather clock crying the hour.

The alarm clock's red numbers confirmed this and now read 3:00 a.m. From downstairs came a squeak, like a forgotten hinge forced to flex. A scream choked in her throat and goose bumps prickled Maddie's arms. The mouse was gone, but spectral paw prints had been left in its wake.

The groaning hinge gave way to measured footsteps that traced a pattern across the wooden floor. Up the hall toward the front door, they moved and paused at the base of the stairs. Maddie swallowed a thick pill of fear. Maybe Mom had woken up and decided to check the door? Before the divorce, she'd often come in and check on them during the night—a tradition Maddie wished she'd start up again. The first stair creaked.

Maddie's paralysis lifted, and she rolled to the right, her hands frantic as she fought to find her sister beneath the covers. "Lena. Lena. Wake up." She dug her nails into Lena's shoulder and shook her. "Lena, please."

Three more stairs protested the early morning hunt. Whoever climbed them was getting closer. Maybe it was Mom. Yet deep down, Maddie knew it wasn't. Mom's pace wasn't so stilted, so haunting.

"Lena." Four more steps groaned. Only a few more and

they'd reach the landing. Maddie pried one of the earbuds out of her sister's ear. "Wake up!"

At last, her sister opened her eyes at the same moment the shuffle of feet padded across the hallway. "What are you doing? Get off me."

Lena pulled her knees up, enacting a barricade between them, and yanked the covers back over her torso. The doorknob rattled, then clicked as the door swung open in a wide arc. Maddie's pulse thrummed, a hummingbird battling against her rib cage. A sludge-like shadow towered in the doorway.

It stood about seven feet tall, and opaque strands of black hair hung from its scalp. Its shoulders were rounded and hunched, as if had endured a lifetime of hard labor. Either that or it had been subjected to an insufferable amount of time confined to a tight space. For a moment, Maddie's terror softened— until it stepped across the threshold. Then she unleashed a horrified scream and dug her nails deep into the exposed flesh of Lena's forearm.

"What the hell?" Lena bolted upright and tried to pry Maddie's fingers out of her skin.

Maddie pointed to the specter with her other hand. "Lena, it's right there!" She didn't look away from the menacing figure and witnessed the precise moment it dematerialized.

Her sister tore her gaze away from her arm, but it was too late. The apparition had dissolved into the shadows, withdrawing to the corners that the night light couldn't reach.

"Have you lost your mind?" Lena asked. "Let go of me." She succeeded in removing Maddie's rigor mortis-grip. Once she was free, she reached over and snapped on the solitary light. "Stop screaming."

Unaware she'd been holding the terror-filled note, Maddie closed her mouth, and a tense silence ballooned.

"Want to tell me what that was all about?"

Maddie turned away from the still open door and hugged Ellie to her chest. "There's something in this house. It was just there. I saw it."

Lena collapsed onto the pillow and glanced at the clock. "Three in the morning? Are you kidding me?"

Tears leaked from Maddie's eyes. "You have to believe me, Lena. I saw it."

A guttural groan growled in Lena's throat. "It was a nightmare. Go back to bed." She reached for the light, but Maddie let out a shrill cry.

"Don't turn it off!" She launched herself across Lena's chest.

Lena scowled and braced her arm to keep Maddie's weight off her. "What is wrong with you? There's nothing there."

Hurried footsteps pounded the stairs, and Maddie latched onto Lena's arm once more. "He's coming back." She tried to dive under the covers and huddle into Lena's side, but her sister pulled away.

"Dude, chill out. It's Mom."

Maddie peeked over the coverlet at the wispy figure standing in the threshold. Gone were the liquid shadows and hunched shoulders. Mom's disheveled bun flopped to the right of her head, and the oversized Looney Tunes tee she'd had since Maddie was three hung haphazardly across her shoulders, the stretched neckline swooping low to expose her collarbone. She gripped the moulding with one hand while she rubbed the sleep from her eyes.

"Girls, do you have any idea what time it is? Stop fighting and go to bed."

"We weren't fighting. Maddie just freaked out."

Lena sat back up and brandished her arm. Dozens of blood-speckled crescents carved her skin. Maddie examined her own fingernails, shocked to discover scarlet beneath the half-moons. Had she really held on to Lena that hard?

"She woke me up screaming about some bad dream."

"It wasn't a dream. There's something bad in this house."

Mom's shoulders fell. For a moment, Maddie saw nothing but a brittle weak woman. How would she be strong enough to keep them safe? "Look, it's three in the morning, and I have to be up in two hours to meet with a woman at the job placement agency. I need you girls to quiet down and get some sleep."

Maddie squeezed her stuffed elephant. "But I saw a man with long black hair. He tried to come into our room."

"Sweetie, it was just a dream. This is a new house in a new place, okay? I know you miss your friends, but—"

"It wasn't a dream. I know what I saw." Maddie's voice wobbled.

Mom let out an exasperated groan. "All right. How about you come sleep with me so your sister can get some rest?"

"Thank you," Lena grumbled and reinserted the earbud Maddie had ripped out.

Mom held out her hand for Maddie to take. With Ellie secured in the crook of her elbow, she glanced over her shoulder at Lena. Part of her felt guilty for leaving her alone. What if the shadow man came back? But her sister had already dismissed her and shut off the light. Now, she was nothing more than a pile of lumpy body parts concealed beneath the thin coverlet. Maddie shuddered as she pictured Lena chopped up and arranged like a dismembered Barbie doll.

"Come on, sweetheart," Mom urged, then closed the door behind them. "Do you want me to carry you, or are you too big for that?"

A small grin tugged at the corner of Maddie's lips, but she declined. Yesterday, she would have jumped at the offer, but not tonight. If the shadow man lurked downstairs, she wanted the floor underfoot and agency over her own body. No one believed her, but she knew what she'd seen. There was no trick of the light and no nightmare. The cold wash of fear had been too real.

Their feet drummed static beats down the aged staircase. Maddie's eyes ping-ponged back and forth as she searched the dark house. They reached the landing at the bottom of the staircase and rounded the banister. Maddie scanned the living room and held her breath. Monsters didn't disappear just because the lights came on. They were too clever for that.

Mom rubbed their joined hands. "Come on. My room is this way, remember? Just past the bathroom."

They ambled down the hall, and Mom's slippers whispered like a dry cough. Chills licked Maddie's spine as they passed the imposing grandfather clock. She slowed her pace and paused in front of the glass façade to stare at the intricate filigree that decorated the face.

It was easy to see the clock's value. Even buried in a blanket of dust, the antique gleamed. It was probably the most expensive piece of furniture in the home. It may have even been worth more than Mom's car. Yet, rather than an air of elegance, the great clock radiated a coldness that extended beyond the typical caution old items demanded of children. It evoked the image of a crusty elderly gentleman who wouldn't hesitate to crack his belt over your backside and then expect a thank-you for curtailing churlish behavior.

Maddie's small hand raised, steered by a compulsion she tried to resist. She didn't want to touch the formidable timepiece, but too soon, the smooth glass was beneath her fingertips. It was just as cold as she'd imagined.

Mom gave their conjoined hands a little shake. "Honey? Are you all right?"

During Maddie's intensive inspection, the monotonous measurement of time crescendoed and dulled all other sound. *Tick. Tock. Tick. Tock.* The brass pendulum swung back and forth like a pendant on a hypnotist's string.

Her mom's muffled voice called to bring her back, but Maddie was transfixed by the *tick- tick-ticking*, cast into a stupor by the intricate song of gears and interlocking cogs. Round and round the tiny machinery spun and drew her gaze to the side, where the smaller hand ticked past the three. Her eyes slid along the whittled brass arrow and across the embellished numeral to rest on a sliver of inky blackness that ran parallel to the length of the chamber. Rich oak wood framed the crevice on the opposite side, but it was incongruent with the left. Weren't clocks supposed to be symmetrical?

Maddie's fingers hovered over the edge of the glass and moved toward the beckoning darkness. Smooth wood nuzzled her fingertips, and warm air enveloped her hand up to her first knuckle. She took a step closer, her desperation to see inside the hidden cavity growing. Her hand touched the frame and pulled, but a hard tug tore her backward and shattered the trance.

A snap of cold air doused her with the force of a bucket of ice water. "What happened?" Maddie asked, wide-eyed.

Mom crouched before her, holding her hips tight. Gone was the exhaustion from her eyes. In its place, Maddie recognized the shallow pools of fear and confusion she'd seen in her own reflection just hours ago.

"Honey, you . . ." Mom's words trailed off, and she sucked in a breath. "Why did you touch the clock? I thought it scared you?"

Maddie bit her lip. "I don't know. It's not so bad when it's quiet."

Mom looked thoughtful. “Did you hear me calling your name?”

Maddie shook her head. “No. The ticking was too loud.” The constant thrum of seconds passing was barely audible now.

“Mads, grandfather clocks don’t keep track of seconds. See? They only have two hands.”

Sure enough, two brass arrows awaited at the end of Mom’s pointed finger, yet even as Maddie took stock of the double-hands, the rhythmic beat of each passing second thudded against her eardrums, as palpable as her own heartbeat.

Seemingly satisfied with her silent acceptance, Mom stood and draped a guiding arm around her shoulders. “It’s really late. Let’s snuggle like we used to.”

Maddie nodded and allowed herself to be led down the hall, the grandfather clock’s distorted shadow leering after her.

CHAPTER 5

"Where's Ellie?" Maddie demanded.

Lena glanced up from her fraction worksheet and fixed her sister with a side eye. "Why would I know where your stupid toy is?"

"She's not stupid. I've been looking for her all day, but she's nowhere."

Lena rolled her eyes. "She's got to be somewhere. She probably fell under the bed." She lowered her head and put her pencil back to the paper. The sound of scratching graphite ended their conversation.

Maddie's shoulders slumped forward. Mom wouldn't be home until the big clock chimed six times. It had been nearly a week in the new house. Thankfully, she hadn't seen any more shadows lurking in alcoves or doorways. She didn't want to admit it, but maybe it had been a dream.

As creepy as the house had been that first night, they'd already fallen into a routine since then. Mom dropped them off at school on her way to work, and the bus returned them around 3:00 p.m. Then they did their homework, and Maddie spent her time exploring the old craftsman while Lena plugged in her headphones and stared at her phone until Mom came home.

After a few days, there wasn't much left to explore, save for the front living room. Mom hadn't had time to box everything up or toss it out yet, and Maddie still couldn't bring herself to enter the space. Untouched after so many years, the inanimate objects resembled a painting, stuck in a limbo as they waited for the artist to complete the portrait. The tea party had been staged; all that was missing were the monsters.

With an exaggerated sigh, Maddie pivoted atop the linoleum and exited the kitchen. Jumping as she walked beneath the threshold, her fingers scraped the top of the painted doorframe. She passed the grandfather clock but barely registered it. The domineering structure still made her uncomfortable, but it no longer emitted the same terrifying force it once had. Either the threat had diminished with the absence of shadows, or her nine-year-old attention span had dismissed the fear to focus on more pressing issues, like how to make friends halfway through the first semester.

Her first few days at school had been uneventful. No one was mean, but they had given her a wide berth that didn't exactly project friendliness. Left alone to execute her search for Ellie until Mom returned, Maddie skipped down the hall toward the stairs. Hopefully, Lena's suggestion about the elephant tumbling beneath the bed would pan out.

She galloped down the hall, and her footfalls changed to a muted thud when she reached the rug in the foyer. She propelled her body around the banister, then stopped cold when a flash of movement winked in her peripheral, accompanied by a metallic clink.

Maddie's long braid swayed with her momentum and brushed her lips before it settled against her collarbone. Arranged in a sitting position, her stuffed elephant was perched on the coffee table, a spiderweb draped teacup before it. She released the carved handrail and took an uneasy step toward the living room.

"Ellie?"

The elephant didn't respond, but its one visible eye stared blankly at her. Maddie toed the entrance to the frozen room. The cold drip of fear she hadn't experienced the last few days returned with startling clarity. She took another step, fully within the living room's reach. The air tasted bitter, like an old penny. She recalled the high-pitched 'tink' she'd heard a moment ago.

Drawn to the coffee table, Maddie sidestepped a dark red pillow that sported gaudy maroon crystal tassels. Curious, she kicked it, but the tassels produced a different sound than the one she hoped to match. She rotated on the balls of her feet toward a decorative spoon that rested at an odd angle against one of the saucers. It lay on its narrow side rather than the flat rounded bowl. She frowned. It looked as if it had slipped off the lip of the plate, but what could have caused it to move?

Perhaps her skips had been too hard? She remembered the plates in the china cabinet back at their old house. Dad was constantly yelling at her to stop running because the floors vibrated and caused the dishware to bounce.

Her fear withdrew. There was always a logical explanation. Maddie's gaze followed the length of the teaspoon as she kneeled beside the table. Prints in the dust trailed away from the utensil like a splattering of tiny raindrops, remnants of spilled tea from a raucous party once upon a time. Maddie's search extended, zigzagging from drop to drop until the circles grew to lines. Swirls turned to hashmarks, then into more intricate drawings. One even depicted a stick figure with long hair. She smiled at the loopy graphics until a sour stone formed in her gut. The markings were fresh. She inhaled a choked gasp. Mom and Lena would never have drawn them, so where had they come from?

She touched the tabletop beneath an illustration with the tip of her nail. No dust clung to her. The drawings were too recent to have even accumulated a fine layer overnight. The stick figures continued down the length of the table, each cartoon becoming more depraved and violent.

The sketches' happy grins fell away to crude circles of terror, and little Xs blotted out the pinpricked eyes. Missing arms and askew necks weighed down with rope caused Maddie's palms to sweat. Was this Lena's idea of a sick joke?

A quiet squeak nearly made Maddie leap to her feet. Sitting on its haunches, in a pose nearly identical to Ellie, was the mouse. She slapped a hand over her heart and exhaled a shaky laugh. "It's just you. How do you keep showing up?"

She shifted her stance so she was eye level with the familiar rodent, but her excitement quickly curdled. Rather than the cute creature she'd expected, up close the mouse resembled a decaying corpse. Mangy patches of pink flesh marred its once lustrous coat, and dried yellow pus stuck to its fur in matted clumps. One eye held her gaze, but the other was clouded with a milky blue discoloration. Suddenly, the mouse dropped to all fours and raced away, skirting cups and dried biscuits caked with the fuzz of turquoise mold.

"Wait. Come back! Do you know who drew these?"

Maddie knew it was ridiculous to ask a rodent for information, but it had appeared three times now. Clearly, it wasn't frightened of them. Had it been alone so long that it wasn't conditioned to fear, or had it known kindness from humans before?

It scurried through a gnawed hole in the coffee table beside a vase of dead wildflowers. The water had long since evaporated, and papery waifs of withered stems and mummified husks of curled leaves clung to the cloudy glass. Maddie followed as the mouse's slim frame slipped through, its long brown tail slithering after. She dropped to her hands and knees to intercept the creature's flight and screamed.

Maddie met a half-emaciated face inches from her own. A young girl lay on her back, but her neck was twisted at an unnatural angle so her lips almost kissed the floor.

Maddie's breath stalled in her throat. Greasy blond hair was matted to the girl's exposed skull, the bone a sickly white like old parchment. Bright red rivulets oozed from the wound, the liquid a sharp contrast to the squishy pink tissue visible beneath the crushed bone. One of her eyes wasn't visible, pressed down on the wooden surface as it was, but the other seemed to bulge out of her head. Her iris had been blue, but the sclera was bloodshot and bruised and had turned a frightening violet color. The eyeball itself had lost its spherical shape, dented and crushed on one side.

The eye kept constant contact with Maddie and stared her down. An incessant *drip-drip-drip* resounded, and warm liquid pooled beneath her palms. She raised them off the floor, and scarlet shrouded her gaze. She rubbed her thumb and forefingers together. The blood was slippery and viscous against the ridges of her fingerprints. The girl's bloodied mouth gaped like a dying fish.

"You'll be next."

The brittle warning wove across the shared space and settled against Maddie's eardrum, as searing as a cattle brand. She glanced back at the whispering corpse and was met with a new pair of eyes, dark brown like her own but rimmed in black kohl. She unleashed another scream.

Daggers cut into her upper arms as the monster rattled her

torso back and forth, spitting ancient words in a tongue she couldn't understand. Maddie fought to get away, fought to pry the claws out of her skin, until the crimson edges dulled at last and her vision revealed Lena by her side. Her face was as white as a sheet as she cried Maddie's name over and over.

"Lena?" Maddie croaked. Lena released her grip on Maddie's arms and pulled her tightly against her chest. "No, stop. There's too much blood."

"What blood?"

Maddie tilted her chin down and saw only the smooth flesh of her palms. "There was a girl. A little dead girl lying under the coffee table. There was blood all over the floor and my hands."

Lena shook her head and regarded her quizzically. "There's no one there, Mads." Her slender brows arched, and Maddie's gut lurched. She recognized that look. It was the same one she'd given her the other night, and it spelled disbelief.

"Why would I make this up?" Maddie gripped her sister's sleeve, desperate to hold her in place until she saw it, too. "Lena, please. The mouse. I saw that mouse again, and—"

A thunderous baritone ricocheted throughout the first floor and drowned out Maddie's pleas. She slammed her hands over her ears and shut her eyes.

"I hate that clock!" Lena spat.

A quartet of chimes followed the first boom until the dominating gongs ceased. The sisters looked at one another, and Lena's expression tickled something in the back of Maddie's mind.

Maddie licked her lips and swallowed the growing lump in her throat. "When we got here that first night, you didn't want to stay here because of Uncle Tommy. What happened in this house?"

Lena's look of concern transformed to dread. Her lips formed a thin line and silence stretched. Maddie opened her mouth to plead with her, but Lena sighed and spoke at last. "He wound up in a psychiatric ward after he brutally murdered his family."

The truth hit Maddie in the gut. "How many kids did he have?"

"He had a wife, our aunt Alice, a little boy named Mason, who was three, and an eight-year-old daughter named Samantha."

A blood-splattered vision punctured Maddie's shaky sense of calm. "How did he kill them?"

Lena shook her head. "I don't know. The cops found him stumbling down the highway covered in blood. He didn't even try to hide the bodies. They charged him with murder, but he was later deemed mentally incompetent to stand trial and sent away."

"We need to talk to him."

"What? No way. He's a psycho killer. Besides, Mom would never take us. She'll kill me if she finds out I even told you."

"She doesn't need to know. We could take a bus."

Lena climbed onto the couch and exhaled loudly. "That's a dumb idea. You have any money for a ticket?"

"No. But we have to find out what happened somehow."

Lena chewed her lip for a second. "I can't search for it on my phone. Mom checks it, and she'd freak." They both considered their options. "The library." Her eyes brightened. "At my school. I can research old newspaper articles."

"What if a teacher sees?"

Lena shrugged. "I'll say it's for a project. They won't question it. Teachers don't care."

Fearful excitement surged through Maddie. She was terrified to uncover the truth, but the only thing worse than not knowing was living in a house brimming with dark and disturbing secrets.

CHAPTER 6

Two days passed before Lena's schedule aligned and she was able to spend her study hall in the library. Maddie's nerves buzzed. Focusing on schoolwork was nearly impossible. In both math and English, her teachers scolded her for not paying attention, and she had to endure two separate lectures on how daydreaming was no way to begin a new career at Ivy Drive Elementary. She listened with glazed eyes. It wasn't easy to do long division with images of a bludgeoned dead girl swirling inside her head, but she didn't bring that up.

After school, the mustard-yellow school bus chugged along its route as the rest of the kids shrieked and traded dirty words they'd caught their parents saying.

Two weeks ago, Maddie would have given anything to be amongst their fervent whispers, but making friends seemed trivial now that she had a haunting to solve.

"Are you the one who lives in the murder house? Hello? Are you deaf?"

Maddie snapped out of her thoughts. "Are you talking to me?"

A young boy hung over the top of the wrinkled brown seat in front of her. His fiery orange curls draped like a mop over his face and parted enough to reveal one inquisitive eye. "So, are you her?"

"Who?"

"The new girl who moved into 11 Creek." A puff of air pushed one of his locks far up his forehead. A splattering of brown freckles peppered his face as if they'd been sprinkled with a heavy hand.

"Yeah, it was my uncle's old house. My family and I just moved in."

"Ew. Your uncle?"

Maddie's face flushed. "Yeah. We moved from out of state. I . . . just found out."

"Have you seen any ghosts? Or blood dripping down the walls? My brother said your uncle killed his whole family, even the pets." The boy licked his lower lip, and bubbles of saliva lingered in the center of the pulpy flesh.

Maddie stared at the run-down grocery store beyond the dirty windowpane. She'd hoped the boy would leave her alone, but her ears perked up at his last word. "They had pets?"

The boy grinned and exposed the gummy gaps that framed his oversized buckteeth. "Two dogs. Their skulls were crushed in with the fireplace poker. I think the girl had a mouse too, but I don't think the cops cared enough to look for it. It probably died of starvation after they cleared out the bodies."

Maddie's stomach churned, threatening to launch her cafeteria-issued cheese pizza. "She had a mouse?"

"Yeah, my brother was in her class. She brought it for show-and-tell one day." The boy narrowed his eyes. "You saw it, didn't you?"

Maddie didn't respond, but she bit her lip nervously.

"No way! There's an actual ghost mouse?"

"Don't be stupid. It's an old house. There's probably a whole nest that moved in while it was vacant." Her tone was dismissive, and she kept the unnatural state of decay the mouse had been in to herself. "Do you know how the little girl died?"

The boy batted an errant curl out of his eyes. "Her dad went nuts. After he killed the dogs, he beat Sam with the same poker and crushed the side of her face." He lightly punched his left temple with his fist and exhaled a loud whoosh of air.

Maddie tried to control her expression as chills assaulted her. The image of the dead girl covered in blood with half her face distorted and fragmented bone exposed lurked behind her eyes. She swallowed, saliva growing thick in her throat. "What about the others?"

The boy shrugged as the bus's brakes squealed to a halt. Maddie recognized the hunched mailbox outside.

"Madison," the driver called. "Your stop, hon."

She slid to the edge of her seat and slung her lime-green backpack over her shoulder.

"See you tomorrow, dead girl. If you survive the night."

Maddie's sneakers hit the pavement. She didn't look behind her as the bus pulled away. She wasn't interested in seeing the two dozen faces staring at the girl who was stupid— or desperate enough— to move into the "murder house."

She walked up the long driveway and tried the handle. It swung open easily, meaning Lena was already home. Maddie dumped her backpack and kicked off her shoes by the foot of the stairs, then headed to the back of the house toward the kitchen. The grandfather clock snarled its customary greeting, but Maddie still flinched as it chimed thrice.

"I hate you, you vile thing."

Maddie opened the glass case and exposed its swinging heart, then slammed it shut with enough force to rattle the frame. A vision of the raucous menace crashing to the floor made her smile, but not even a hairline fracture appeared in the glass to reward her efforts.

Lena tipped back in her chair and poked her head around the doorframe. "Easy there, slugger."

Maddie groaned and stomped into the kitchen. "I just wish it would break." She fell onto one of the stools and cupped her chin in her hands.

Lena nodded and drifted back to the numerous papers scattered across the table. "I get that, but look . . . I found all these articles about the house and Uncle Tommy today."

Maddie's disparaging mood evaporated. She sat ramrod straight, as if she'd been shocked. "A boy on the bus told me how Samantha died. Her dad beat her head in with a fire poker."

Lena nodded. "I learned that, too. The guy was sick. Aunt Alice also suffered blunt force trauma, but she was still alive, so the twisted bastard filled up the tub and drowned her."

Maddie recalled the dark shadow crouched in the corner of the shower that first night. Was that the ghost of their aunt? "What about the little boy?"

Lena shuffled the papers and winced. "His was the worst. He managed to get outside. He ran to the edge of the road to flag someone down, but Uncle Tommy . . ." She looked up from the apparently graphic retelling.

"Tell me. I can handle it." Maddie wished she looked older. Wished her limbs weren't so gangly and that her hair didn't hang limp in front of her face. She wished she didn't need a stuffed animal to feel safe. She wished she didn't sound so scared. "I promise. I need to know."

Lena pursed her lips but gave in. "Yeah, I think you do." She stacked the papers, careful to keep the ones with the grainy black-and-white images concealed. "Mason made it to the road and was trying to flag someone down. There was a report from a motorist that night. He said he saw a little boy crying and waving his arms. Before he could pull over, Uncle Tommy reversed down the driveway in his car. He . . . he didn't stop. The witness described Tommy speeding down the drive until the bumper slammed into Mason. He kept driving until the car crashed into the mailbox. The post wedged under the tire, and Mason's body was pinned between the trunk and the metal pole. His spine snapped from the impact."

Revulsion churned Maddie's stomach. How could a father bludgeon and run down his own children? Her shoulders quivered. The hunched figure she'd seen out by the road . . . She wasn't seeing things. The house was overrun with spirits.

"What did Uncle Tommy say? Did he say why he did it?"

Lena flipped through several papers. "When they arrested him, he claimed he was innocent."

Maddie gasped. "What?"

"Yup, the scumbag. He raved about something called 'The Keeper,' which had apparently marked and killed his family, but none of the detectives or psychologists could determine what or who he meant, so he was sent to Dixon Summit State Hospital in Cheyenne."

"Marked? Keeper? What does that mean?"

Lena shrugged. "How the hell should I know? The guy was a nut who murdered his whole family. People like that don't need a reason, they just snap."

"I wish we could talk to him. Hear it in his own words."

Lena hissed through her teeth. "I already told you it's a dumb idea. Now, come on. Help me clean this up before Mom gets home."

CHAPTER 7

Hours later, Maddie lay in bed curled on her side with Ellie in her arms. Her sleep had been restless, too full of gruesome renditions of the house's disturbed history. When she finally fell into a deep slumber, Samantha's bloodied face awaited her. She tried to wake herself up, but the vision held firm. Sam's uninjured eye blinked while blood trickled from the other's crushed socket.

"Maddie," the ghost said. "You need to leave this house. I don't have much time before he wakes."

"Who?"

"The Keeper. He measures time and takes more than his share to ensure he reigns immortal."

The familiar name nearly jolted Maddie awake. "Why are you scaring me?"

Samantha shook her head. Her greasy hair parted to reveal the exposed brain tissue beneath her concave skull. "To keep you safe. The Keeper is growing weak. The last soul he claimed is dying. He needs a new source."

"A new source of what?"

"Life to fuel his immortality. The Keeper grows more desperate each day. If his vessel dies, he won't be able to keep control of the spirits he's marked. The energy he absorbed from our souls would evaporate. My mom, brother, and I would be free, and he would cease to exist. You must leave."

Maddie glanced away from the girl's worried mouth. "But my mom just got a new job and . . . we don't have anywhere else to go."

Sam sighed. "Then two of you will join us."

Maddie's gut lurched. "Join you? We're going to die?"

"Not all of you."

"What does that mean?"

The grandfather clock roared downstairs. The triplet chimes wormed into Maddie's brain. Sam's eye bulged. "He's coming. I have to go. He can't know I spoke to you. Don't tell your sister. He'll hear. He'll know I told."

"Wait. How do I stop him?"

Sam hung her head. "You can't. Get your family as far away as you can, and if he does catch you, hold a mirror in front of your face. It's the only way to hide."

The dream dissolved and left Maddie bathed in a cold sweat. The grandfather clock chimed for the third and final time, followed by the unmistakable groan of the clock's heavy façade swinging open on ancient hinges.

Maddie's eyes popped open. The Keeper that Uncle Tommy had raved about. The shadow man she'd seen on their maiden night. They were one and the same.

Footsteps creaked down the hall, but Maddie lost track of the shadow man as he transitioned to the oriental runner that ran from the bathroom to Mom's bedroom. Her heart jackhammered in its cage. She had no idea of the man's motives, but from Sam's warning and the growing unease in her gut, she knew they were sinister.

Part of her wanted to rush downstairs and protect her mom. Was he stalking her? Getting ready to kill them tonight? But the thought of facing him alone and defenseless froze her to the mattress with her mind stuck on a vicious spin cycle.

The landing just outside her door groaned, and too late Maddie realized she had been so preoccupied that she'd missed the shadow man's ascent. Sam's warning broke through her terror. She needed to find a mirror. Lena's purse perched on the edge of their shared dresser like a roosting hen.

Maddie scuffled off the bed and swiped the clutch from its stand, but it tumbled to the carpet. Leaping down to her hands and knees, she rooted around on the dark floor until her fingertips brushed the cool silver compact Lena carried around at school. The doorknob turned, and the door swung inward too quietly to have been operated by a corporeal being. Maddie stifled a choked sob as the inky black shadow billowed into the room with long purposeful strides. The Keeper picked up his legs, his knees level with his stomach, while his arms waved like fluttering ribbons.

Maddie frowned. He certainly didn't seem weak like Sam had described. Waltzing forward, the Keeper sidled up to the side of their shared bed. Lena dreamed, blind and deaf to the terrifying creature inches away. Maddie tried to move, but before she could muster the courage, the shadow man raised one of his elongated arms and flexed his spidery fingers.

Globs of sticky web dangled from his fingers, and Maddie's teeth chattered as the Keeper brushed his hand along the back of Lena's neck. A quiet hiss sizzled like rain hitting hot asphalt, followed by a red-orange spark, similar to the end of a cigarette flaring to life as he dragged his nail across her vulnerable skin. A horrified squeak escaped Maddie's lips before she could smother it. What she assumed was the Keeper's hand snapped in her direction. Long wispy tendrils floated about his head like Medusa's snakes sniffing her out.

The pads of Maddie's fingertips mashed down on the compact, and suddenly she remembered why she held it in the first place. The shadow man didn't waste time skirting around the width of the bed; instead, he raised his long legs and stepped right over Lena onto the mattress. Maddie's chest grew tight as the coverlet depressed around the impact of his shadowy foot. Step over step, his strange gait carried him closer until he leered like a gargoyle over a parapet. Her fingers fumbled to undo the compact's clasp. Terror stalled the breath in her throat, and her sweat-slicked palms nearly caused the accessory to slip. The Keeper breathed through his mouth, the sound eerily reminiscent of a ticking clock.

At last, Maddie's fingers worked the clasp apart, and the mirror opened. His monotonous breaths veered closer. Her sister was now entirely cloaked in shadow. Maddie couldn't be sure if Lena was still lying in bed or if the creature had sent her to some distant dimension. Sam's warning blared in her mind again. The mirror was the only way to hide. The shadow man's noxious exhales grew louder and came close enough to warm her cheeks, shattering her paralysis, and she jerked the open compact before her face with a whispered prayer on her lips. Sam hadn't specified how large the mirror had to be, but this was her only hope.

Her hand shook, and she pressed herself against the dresser, but she didn't dare close her eyes. If she did, they might not ever open again. Maddie peered over the rim of the compact's frame and tried not to move. Several floating strands of his hair disturbed the air above her head; one even brushed the halo of fine hairs that framed her own face. Her hand quaked. Why wasn't it repelling him?

A raspy voice that sounded older than time itself slithered out of the darkness. "I can smell you, child. Where are you?

Where have you hidden?" Maddie angled the compact to the left.

The Keeper snarled as the mirror captured his reflection. "Little witch. You won't be able to escape me for long. Two have been marked. You're running out of time."

A chilling breeze rippled through the small bedroom. Maddie held her pose. Her whole arm shook now. She wouldn't be able to hold it for much longer. The shadow man growled, and the sound reverberated in her chest.

He rushed from the room, his shadow-dripped limbs snapping like an agitated raven taking flight. The murky shadows coalesced and dove through the door. Gone was his grace.

Maddie lowered the mirror as the Keeper bolted down the stairs. She didn't understand his urgency. He'd retreated as if he were the one being hunted. She rose from her curled position on the floor and gripped the mattress for stability. That's when she received her answer.

The clock chimed four sharp bursts, but something was off. Rather than the drawn-out gongs, it sounded angry, like it couldn't announce the hour fast enough. Because time needed its Keeper.

An idea began to take form as Maddie slunk under the covers. Part of her itched to shut the door, but what did it matter when it did nothing to keep out the monsters? Besides, his time to torment was over. The Keeper was bound to the ticking clock, just like the rest of them.

CHAPTER 8

"Lena! Lena!" Maddie cried as soon as her feet hit the driveway. There hadn't been time to talk that morning, but now that they'd reached the end of the school day, they had a solid three hours before Mom got off work.

She raced inside. Her sister had seemed fine that morning as all three of them shuffled through their morning routines and jostled for use of the bathroom. Lena had been unfriendly and grumpy, but that wasn't anything new.

"Lena, where are you?"

Maddie scoured Lena's usual haunts, but both the kitchen and their room were empty. Had her sister stayed after school? She exited the swinging door of the kitchen and headed back down the hall. The grandfather clock towered above her, its eyeless face seeing everything.

It read 3:07. Maddie took a steadying breath and advanced closer. The heavy feeling of being watched descended, inescapable and suffocating. She knew the Keeper lurked within and followed every step she took while encased in his wooden prison. A surge of bravery bloomed in her chest, and she narrowed her eyes.

"I'm going to stop you."

The back door slammed and shook Maddie from her

stupor. She blinked and raced toward the kitchen to find Lena standing in front of the fridge.

"Lena!" Maddie ran over and wrapped her arms around her sister's waist. "I thought he took you."

Lena dislodged an earbud. "What are you talking about? Took me where?"

Maddie arched her neck. "The Keeper. He came into our room last night, and when I got off the bus, I couldn't find you."

Lena pushed away Maddie's squid-like grip. "Chill out. I was taking out the garbage. Who came into our room?" She opened the fridge and withdrew a red Gatorade.

Maddie dropped her voice. "The man who lives in the clock."

Lena unscrewed the cap and took a generous swig, then paused, resting the bottle against her lip. "Hold on, the Keeper? That's the name Uncle Tommy kept telling the cops. What's going on?"

"You won't believe me."

Lena fixed her with a hard stare and lowered the bottle. "Just tell me."

"Okay." Maddie wrung her hands in front of her. "Do you remember our cousin Samantha who was bludgeoned?"

"How many other cousins do we have that have been murdered with a fireplace poker?"

Maddie ignored her comment. "I had a dream about her last night. Actually, it was more like she came to me in the dream."

"Still waiting for any information of value."

"Listen. In my dream, Sam told me the Keeper is real. Remember the shadow in our room I saw our first night? That's him."

Lena frowned. "But a shadow can't hurt you."

"This one can. It opened the clock and our door. It has

enough weight to make the floorboards creak. Please believe me, Lena. Uncle Tommy wasn't making it up. What if he didn't kill his family?"

"Come on, Mads. This doesn't make any sense. You had another nightmare. That's all."

Maddie crossed her arms. "I did not. I know what I saw. Sam told me—" Her eyes widened, and her mouth tightened into a small O.

"What?"

"She told me not to tell you."

Lena wrinkled her nose. "Who? The dead girl?"

"Sh, sh, sh." Maddie fluttered her hands before her face and motioned to the back door. "Outside."

Lena stood her ground, but Maddie pushed her along. Together, they shuffled through the door onto the concrete slab outside, overrun with splintering cracks and thick weeds.

"What is wrong with you, Mads? Why are we out—"

"He'll hear us. Sam warned me not to speak of it. The Keeper is always listening."

"Give me a break."

Lena tried to nudge her aside, but Maddie held firm. "You have to believe me. We need to get out of here as soon as Mom gets back."

"We just finished unpacking. Plus, we don't have anywhere else to go. You're being paranoid. I knew I shouldn't have shared those articles with you."

Maddie stamped her foot. "We're going to die, Lena! Doesn't that mean anything to you?"

Lena rolled her eyes and looked up at the darkening sky. "We're not going to die."

"Yes, we are. We're going to end up just like Sam and her family if we stay."

"Enough! They died because there was something wrong with Uncle Tommy. He killed them. Not some sadistic shadow thing that lives in a clock. Do you realize how dumb you sound?"

Maddie set her lips in a thin line. Tears pricked the backs of her eyes, but she refused to cry. She didn't want to give her sister the satisfaction. Plus, there wasn't time to fight. "Why were all the mirrors gone when we moved in? Everything else was left as it was but all the mirrors were stashed in the office Uncle Tommy used."

Lena shrugged. "So? Someone who managed the estate probably took them down to start cleaning or something."

Maddie shook her head and dropped her voice even lower. "Sam told me mirrors are the only way to hide from him. What if Uncle Tommy figured it out and tried to stop him, but he—"

"Killed them all instead?" Lena finished, her tone skeptical.

Maddie chewed the inside of her cheek. There was a piece missing, and it danced just out of reach. Something else she needed to remember. Lena sighed and gathered her long black hair off the back of her neck and piled it on top of her head. A small red symbol peeked out from behind her ear. Maddie's jaw dropped.

"When did you get a tattoo? Mom's going to flip."

"What are you talking about, egghead? I don't have a tattoo."

"Did you cut yourself?" Maddie pointed.

"On my neck? How would I do that?"

Maddie shrugged and peered closer. It didn't look like a cut. It looked more like a brand. The image of the Keeper looming over her sister, accompanied by the sizzling hiss, flashed in her mind. Maddie's hands flew to her mouth.

"The Keeper. He did that to you last night."

"Did what?" Lena ran her fingertips along her skin until she grazed the small symbol tucked just below her hairline. "What is this? Quick, take a picture." She handed Maddie her phone and held her hair up farther.

Maddie zoomed in and clicked the white button in the center of the screen before she turned it to Lena. "Look."

Lena accepted the phone and studied the photo, worrying her bottom lip between her teeth. She traced the intricate carving with a finger, and at last, she spoke. "Do you remember the police report? How Uncle Tommy was adamant that the Keeper had killed his family?"

Maddie nodded. "What about it?"

"That wasn't the only thing he accused the Keeper of doing." Lena tapped her neck. "He claimed this thing had marked them, too."

CHAPTER 8

Maddie's mouth hung open, and her lip quivered. "So this . . . this is happening again?"

Lena paled, and the black eyeliner she had caked on that morning stood out even more starkly, her face resembling a beautiful skull.

"He stayed downstairs for a while last night before he came to our room. We have to check if he marked Mom," Maddie said when Lena didn't answer.

"Where's your mark? Does it look like this?"

Maddie shook her head. "He tried, but he couldn't find me. I hid behind that compact mirror you had in your purse."

Lena snorted. "Well, it was nice of you to help me." Her long hair fell like a curtain back into place. The brand was no longer visible, but the weight of its presence was hard to ignore.

Maddie grabbed her hand and squeezed. "I'm sorry. I wanted to cover us both, but I was too scared."

Lena wrapped her in a tight hug. "It's okay. This isn't your fault." She exhaled a long breath. "I can't believe this is happening . . . Why did this ghost thing choose us?"

Maddie knew she didn't expect an answer, but there was more to it than bad luck. "It's not a ghost that just happened upon us. More like we happened upon him. He's tied to the grandfather clock. Sam said he's running out of energy. He needs to attach himself to a new soul."

"A new soul? That's why he needs to kill us?"

"No. Sam said only two of us were going to die. He chooses one to become his vessel and then absorbs the other souls to heighten his energy. That's why the Keeper didn't kill all of them before."

"Uncle Tommy," Lena whispered. "The killings gave the Keeper power, but he's a leech. He can only survive as long as his host is healthy."

"We need to get the name of the facility they took Uncle Tommy to and check on him. It might tell us how much time we have left." Maddie pulled open the door, but Lena slammed it shut.

"We can't go back in there. You said it yourself. He'll hear."

"Not if we don't talk. We'll find the articles and then come back outside to make the call."

Lena shivered and glanced at her phone. "Okay. It's 3:51 p.m. We have to hurry. Mom will be here soon."

Maddie nodded and gripped the handle once more. Before she opened it, she turned over her shoulder to look at her sister. "Thanks for believing me."

Lena grinned. "You're welcome. Let's go."

They walked back into the house. There was no need to sneak; the shadow man already knew they were onto him. Lena led the way to their room. As they passed the grandfather clock, the pendulum seemed to growl, conjuring images of a caged tiger pacing the bars of its cell until feeding hour. Maddie tried to subdue her shiver, but it rolled through her body with unstoppable force. Lena climbed the stairs while tracing the mark on her neck. No doubt she felt the eerie sense that radiated through the home as well.

They hurried to the top of the landing, and Lena veered to her side of the room where her backpack lay by the bed. She dragged it out, unzipped it, and reached in. Her face scrunched in concentration, and after a few wrong attempts, she withdrew the correct paper. She waved Maddie over as she did her best to smooth the wrinkles out of the crumpled sheet. Maddie followed her sister's finger to the line in the article that detailed the name of facility: Dixon Summit State Hospital. Hope fluttered in her chest. They could do this.

Lena held up her phone and nodded toward the door. With the article clutched in her hand, they traversed downstairs and rounded the banister toward the back of the kitchen. Maddie's steps were light, and for the first time since she'd entered the house, she smiled. The end of the nightmare was in sight. As long as Uncle Tommy was alive, they had a chance to get out and end the terrifying cycle. Without a healthy host to manipulate, the monster had no choice but to shrivel and die.

They hurried down the hall. Lena's screen flared to life as she typed the hospital's name. The clock screamed, the chimes like violent claps of thunder.

"Oh, shit." Lena flinched. Her phone dropped from her palm and slid under the clock's feet, disappearing into the cavernous void beneath. "No!"

Maddie dropped to her hands and knees and peered into the dusty blackness. She could see the phone, the screen still active. It was only a foot away. She could reach it. Maddie stuck the tips of her fingers into shadow, but an icy hand closed around her ankle and jerked her back.

"Lena, stop. I can get it."

"I didn't do anything."

Maddie glanced behind her and shrieked. A semi-corporeal apparition crouched against the wall. It was female. Water droplets clung to her long hair, and her sallow skin looked slightly bloated. The frigid touch released, and the image blinked before vanishing completely.

Lena whipped her head around, but the ghost was gone. "What is it?"

Maddie pressed a finger to her lips and gestured to the kitchen. She pushed herself to her feet.

"But my phone . . ."

"Leave it."

Lena frowned but followed Maddie into the kitchen, and they retreated to the yard once again as the fourth chime gonged. She rounded on Maddie the second the door clicked shut. "What the hell? How are we supposed to call the hospital? Why didn't you grab the phone?"

"I'm sorry. I started to, but then I felt something touch my ankle. I saw Aunt Alice. She stopped me from reaching under the clock."

Lena crossed her arms. "Why? It doesn't have teeth."

"I don't know, but the ghosts are on our side."

"Shit. What do we do now? We can't just sit here and wait for that creepy thing to come out. It's almost dark. Do you suggest we start walking and hope we stumble upon a neighbor?"

Light flakes twirled in the open air, but the snowfall didn't fill Maddie with excitement. Instead, it felt foreboding, as if it would bury them by morning. "We do what we should have done the first night. If he lives in the clock, then we need to destroy it."

Lena shivered and drew her arms around her torso. "Won't that just release him faster?"

"I don't think so. He's bound to the clock. If we break it, he'll be trapped inside every broken piece."

Lena dragged her hand down her face and let out a defeated

sigh. "I guess we don't have much choice. All right. Let's find something to smash it with."

Maddie smirked. "I know the perfect weapon."

CHAPTER 10

The fire poker was heavy in Maddie's hands, but the weight felt reassuring. Still, the dark brown flakes that rubbed off churned her stomach. She imagined Samantha's skull caving in under the sharp blows, her blood running down the shaft. As twisted as it was, she was glad the police had left it behind. It was the perfect poetic justice.

She bounced the poker in her palm. "You ready?"

Beside her, Lena worried her hands around the trunk of an old wooden baseball bat they'd found in the garage. "Yeah. Let's do this. You want the first swing?"

Maddie nodded and slid her hands down the length of the poker until she had a firm grip. Lena backed up to allow her plenty of room and held the bat at the ready in case the Keeper jumped out. Maddie sunk into a semi-crouched stance and gritted her teeth, remembering the day she had opened the clock's chest and slammed it as hard as she could. The glass hadn't shattered then, but she prayed the wrought iron bite of the fire poker would prove more successful.

With a quick inhale, Maddie rotated her shoulders and swung the poker with all the fury she could muster. The curved tip smashed the glass just as the front door unlocked.

"Madison Amelia! What the hell are you doing?" Her

mother raced inside and threw her purse on the floor.

The glass hadn't broken. Instead, the poker had become wedged in the transparent front. Maddie wriggled it back and forth to dislodge it and was rewarded by the quiet tinkling of glass.

"Mom, stay back. You don't understand!" she cried.

"She's right. We have to do this," Lena said, defending Maddie, but Mom shook her head and stormed toward them.

She knocked the bat down to a neutral position and stepped in front of the clock, blocking it from their rampage. Maddie yanked the poker free right before her mother crossed her path.

"That is enough. I won't stand by while you destroy our home."

"Mom, listen to us—"

"Stop. I know you both hate it here and hate this old thing." Mom jerked her thumb over her shoulder. Even though the glass had a sizeable gash, the pendulum continued to swing. "But if you're angry, we talk about it. We don't smash the house apart."

"Mom, please—" Lena started, but their mom fixed her with a grim look.

She rubbed her eyes and unleashed a bone-deep sigh. "I didn't sleep well last night, work was a nightmare, and on my way home, I found out my brother passed away this afternoon."

Maddie's gaze connected with Lena's. The terror that swelled in her chest was reflected in her sister's eyes. "Uncle Tommy?"

"Yes. The hospital called because I was listed as next of kin."

Maddie swallowed the thickening lump in her throat. They were out of time. They had to convince Mom to leave immediately; otherwise, Samantha's prophecy would come true.

"Now, clean this up and put those ridiculous things outside." Mom ran her fingers through her disheveled ponytail and closed her eyes.

"Okay, Mom," Lena answered, but Maddie didn't move. A bright red scratch on her mother's wrist caught her eye as she moved her hand from her hair.

"What happened?" Maddie pointed to her mother's injured arm.

Mom lowered her hand and drew back her sleeve. Maddie's stomach clenched. "I'm not sure. I must have cut it at work."

Maddie narrowed her eyes. It was too similar in color to the mark behind Lena's ear to be a coincidence. Two of them had been branded by the Keeper, chosen for death. She felt Lena stiffen by her side and knew she'd seen the mark as well.

"Mom, we need to get in the car and leave right now," Maddie explained.

Mom wandered back to the front door. It stood open to the gathering snow beyond. A smooth white blanket already covered the grass.

"Honey, there's a big storm rolling in. We'll have leftovers tonight and watch a movie, okay?" Mom gripped the edge of the door and began to close it, but not before Maddie's gaze alighted on Mason's ghost in the distance.

Horror twisted his little face as he beckoned them outside. The sky was nearly pitch black, but out there, at least they stood a chance.

"You don't understand. We can't stay here. It's not safe."

Mom sighed again and picked up her purse from the floor. Her cell phone had fallen onto the hardwood, and she tucked it into one of the pockets on the leg of her scrubs.

"We can go to a motel. We'll explain everything there," Lena added.

"A motel? Guys, I can't afford that." Their mother's tone grew rough. She pointed to the weapons in their hands. "And I told you to put those outside. What is going on with you two tonight?"

Maddie tried to corral her mom toward the door, the fire poker still clutched in her fists. "We'll tell you at the motel. Get in the car. He's coming!"

"Who?"

"The Keeper!" Lena shouted. She glanced at the stoic clock, but Mom held her ground.

"Girls, I don't have time for this—"

"None of us do. We're all out of time and—"

The rest of Maddie's sentence was drowned out by a thunderous melody. The long hand ticked into the upright position, preparing to announce the new hour and possibly unleash the Keeper within.

The grandfather clock rocked back and forth, shaking atop the floor. Maddie tore her gaze away from her mom and raised the iron poker. A small gray object clung to the crown of the timepiece before it darted around the back, its long tail waving like a flag as the mouse ran down the clock. Lena copied her movements. Dread wormed into Maddie's gut. She didn't want to hurt the tiny animal, but they couldn't delay. Together, she and Lena spun, and their weapons tore through the air before Mom could stop them.

Harder and harder they swung. Lena attacked the glass case while Maddie hacked at the wooden sides. The incessant gongs bellowed louder— the mechanism's final plea for mercy— but the girls didn't stop. Not until the clock's cries quieted and the once elegant antique was reduced to splinters and broken shards.

Maddie stepped back. Her shoulders heaved with exertion.

Lena wiped sweat off her upper lip, and their mother released a bewildered gasp. Maddie paid her no mind. She was far too concerned with examining the contents of the decimated clock now that they'd spilled its innards. The face was still largely in one piece, the hands poised at five o'clock.

No shadows poured forth. No demonic voices chimed like a nettling bell.

"Is it over?" Lena asked.

Maddie kicked the dented brass pendulum, and several gears skittered across the floorboards. "I guess so." She continued to search as a nagging sensation pulled at the back of her mind, as if something were hiding in plain sight.

She froze as the mange-covered mouse popped out of the wreckage, tilted its head in her direction, and blinked its milky eyes. Agitated squeaks punctuated the air, and Maddie watched, transfixed, as he scampered away as fast as his legs could carry him.

"Great. I hope you two have a very good explanation for all of this—" Mom's eyes grew wide, and her face turned chalky.

Maddie had been so focused on the mouse that she hadn't noticed the way the shadows fled the corners to coalesce into one large veil against the wall where the clock had once stood. Maddie studied the grandfather's shadow. It painted the wallpaper as if the clock still stood.

"What is that?" Mom whispered.

Maddie's breath caught in her throat as she realized she'd been fooled again. Without warning, the crisp shadow exploded into the Keeper's elongated dripping form and launched itself forward.

CHAPTER 11

"Run!" Maddie heaved the heavy iron toward the thickest part of the shadow. Her foot slipped on a piece of the ruined case, and she fell to the floor just as the Keeper sailed overhead. Her mother screamed and stumbled backward out the front door that was still ajar. "No!"

The hurtling shadow shoved her down, and the back of her head slammed against the cold brick porch. Maddie stabbed the poker into the floorboards and used it to pull herself up, but Lena was already there. She watched in awe as her sister swung the wooden bat with a rage she'd never witnessed from her before. It sliced through the inky blackness and sent charcoal splatter against the walls with a squelching smack.

The Keeper stretched toward the ceiling, bobbing and weaving around Lena's hits, but it looked as if its responses were slowing. Lena screamed and swung directly toward the center of the Keeper's headlike shape. A sickening crack resounded, and she dropped the bat with a cry of pain.

Maddie didn't know if the Keeper had bitten the bat in half or if Lena had overestimated her swing and accidentally connected with the wall, but the bat clattered to the floor, the ravaged end now a bouquet of lethal wooden fangs.

Her mother hadn't moved; the blow had knocked her out

cold. Lena couldn't drive, and even if they managed to back down the driveway, the roads were too slick to go anywhere. They couldn't get out, but maybe someone could reach them. The memory of her mom tucking her phone into her pocket bloomed. They could call for help.

"Lena! Get Mom's phone. Call the police."

Lena dodged a wispy tentacle-like limb and patted Mom's legs. The Keeper growled wetly and slunk closer. His giant form nearly shrouded her sister completely. Maddie gripped the fire poker and ran at full force. It was her turn. With an animalistic cry, she charged.

The Keeper flicked out a long arm that cracked through the air like a whip. Ducking, Maddie raised the poker lever with her ear, then threw it like a javelin. It whistled and struck the wall, pinning the Keeper's shoulder in place.

Below him, Lena found the phone and slid it free before opening the dial pad. She punched in the numbers and put it to her ear. "It's ringing!"

"Good. We can get out of here!"

The Keeper roared, as if outraged by her announcement. The shadows grew around the poker, convulsing. It took Maddie a second to realize he was trying to tear himself free.

"Help! Help! We need help. It's trying to kill us!" Lena shouted into the phone. "Our address is 11 Creek—"

The Keeper unleashed another demonic rasp, but this time, it was accompanied by a metallic cacophony as the fire poker ripped free from the plaster and dented the wooden planks beneath. Before Maddie could utter a sound, he thrashed his arms and punched Lena in the side, sending her somersaulting into the living room. Her sister let out a shrill yell and dropped the phone, crashing atop the coffee table. Dishes and teacups scattered in a wave of fragmented porcelain.

"Lena!"

The Keeper fixed his sights on Maddie and shrank in height. The elongated arms hung off him, but rather than a ravaging beast, he seemed to compose himself as he sauntered down the foyer.

"Get away from me."

A sticky laugh emanated from the shadow man. "I need you, Madison. We're all running out of time, but you can save me." Black tendrils floated around his head, and his fingers drooped as he lifted his arm. "You can let me in willingly and share my power, or—"

"Leave me and my family alone!"

The Keeper cocked his head. "Then I'll take your soul by force and devour your mind until you're as crazed as the last one."

Uncle Tommy.

The lights sputtered. Maddie glanced at the chandelier overhead, and her heart raced. "No, no. Please, no." But the house had no interest in her pleas, and each sconce extinguished, plunging her into darkness. A buzzing sound followed, and the lights re-illuminated a moment later, but the Keeper was gone.

Maddie scanned the empty hall, her breaths raspy and shallow as her heart rate increased. She needed Ellie to combat the rising panic.

Without the constant ticking of the clock, it felt as if time itself had suspended.

Her mother groaned and shifted her leg. She lay across the threshold, and winter's icy bite swirled inside. Maddie took a step. They could still escape. "Mom—"

A slick oily hand slapped over Maddie's lips before she could cry out. Dozens of fingers that tasted of metal and grease pried open her teeth and reached down her throat. She gagged and clawed at the invading appendage, but her nails slipped on its evasive surface.

A sinister voice gnashed in her ear. “We could have shared, young one. Now, I will take all of you.”

Maddie fought to kick free, but the Keeper held her steady. Vomit climbed her throat as his hands poured into her body and forced the bile back down. Her body seized, completely at the mercy of the shadows. Her eyes rolled, and she caught the silhouette of three figures. At first, she thought her mom and sister had risen, but then she recognized the bludgeoned face of Sam standing between her family. Grim looks painted their faces, and rather than the corporal beings they had presented themselves as earlier, all of them were now translucent, as insubstantial as vapor.

“Sorry, Maddie. I tried to warn you. You should have left. Don’t worry. We’ll watch over them,” Sam said.

Maddie was desperate to ask what she meant, but the Keeper wasn’t through with her. He shoved even more of his essence down her throat and into her nose. Choked gasps rained from her lips, and she fell to her knees. The trio of ghosts simply stood and watched.

Maddie didn’t know how much of the shadow she had ingested, but she felt as if she might burst. Her stomach distended, and her throat burned from the friction. Her eyes rolled into the back of her head as her lips closed at last, and her small body collapsed to the floor with a muted thud.

CHAPTER 12

Maddie's eyelids peeled back. She lay on the broken heap of wood from the damaged clock and groaned as a large shard pierced her thigh. She tried to sit up but couldn't. She had no agency over her body, as if the tether between her mind and limbs had been sliced. She could only watch, a passenger. Someone else was in control.

Strange, isn't it? a familiar voice hissed in her mind. *Observing yourself without the ability to manipulate muscle or bone?*

Maddie shouted as loudly as she could. "Lena!" Her own hand slammed over her mouth and cut off the scream.

Ah, ah. None of that. You may be able to speak, but trust me, it won't do you any good.

The Keeper pushed Maddie to her feet and strolled gaily toward the front door. She couldn't feel anything. Not her swinging arms or the floor beneath her shoes. She was a specter, forced to travel where the shadow man led and only see only where he looked, and right now, he had his sights set on her mother's stirring form.

"Leave her alone!" Maddie cried, but her words were incomprehensible babble behind her hand.

Silly child. That's not how this works. I marked her for a reason. I prefer my vessels to be older, more controlled, but you have so much energy. Such vitality. You will make me strong.

"No!"

The demon only laughed. *You don't have a choice, my dear.*

The Keeper stepped outside and crouched over her mother's body. Her eyelids fluttered with consciousness. Keeping one hand over her mouth, Maddie was helpless to stop herself from reaching for one of the loose bricks that rested at the edge of the porch. She screamed herself hoarse, but her mom couldn't hear her pleas.

What would have been heavy for Maddie, the Keeper lifted with ease as he positioned the brick above her mom's forehead. Maddie wailed again, but instead of tightening his grip over her mouth, the Keeper dropped her hand to grip the brick with both hands.

"Mom! Mom, wake up! Please, Mom. It's not me! It's not me!"

Her mom rubbed her eyes and looked at Maddie, confused. "Honey, what happened? What are you—" She paused when she noticed the brick in her hand. "Honey?"

"Mommy, I'm sorry! It's not me!"

The Keeper brought her arms down and angled the brick so the broad side connected first. He smashed it against the pale skin between her mother's eyebrows, and a sickening thud echoed. Her mom's hands waved frantically, trying to fight her off, but the Keeper slammed the brick again and again, reducing her mother's beautiful face to ground meat and bashed bone.

Tears ran down Maddie's face in direct contrast with the ferocious flailing of her limbs. "Mommy! Mommy, no! I'm sorry!"

Her mom stopped fighting back, and blood splattered Maddie's face, but the Keeper didn't stop. Bone crunched. Her mother's skull and face were an unrecognizable bloody mess. Pink brain matter seeped out of the cracked plates and puddled against Maddie's knee.

"Mommy! Mommy!"

At last, the brick rolled out of her hands. The Keeper didn't watch it fall. Instead, he kept her eyes trained on the pulpy mass that used to be her mother.

"Why did you do that? My mommy . . ."

Maddie yearned to collapse forward and hold her mom, but the Keeper's posture was inflexible. Tears mingled with blood, coursed down her face and neck. She wished she could close her eyes, but even that small mercy he denied.

Watch, child.

Cloudy white vapor lifted from her mom's chest like hot steam after a shower. The Keeper leaned forward and inhaled the rising mist, absorbing every droplet. Once he'd captured it all, their shared body shuddered, and a rush of euphoria rippled down her spine.

Souls elicit the most delicious high, and each one gives us more strength. Don't you see? Their sacrifice keeps us strong.

"Maddie?" A small voice whispered from inside the house. Hope rose in her chest, but it quickly soured when the Keeper chuckled.

Your mother's soul was a start, but imagine the power your sister's will yield.

"Lena, run!" Maddie tried to scream, but her voice was thick and muffled. With the capture of her mother's soul, the Keeper was even more indomitable. He still allowed her to speak but regulated the tone, volume, and emotion now. As she called to Lena, her words became flat and hollow, though tears still lined her face.

He forced her to stand and reenter the house, and Maddie caught a glimpse of her reflection in the glass design of the door. She was covered in far more blood than she'd thought, and with the tracks of her tears, it looked as if the flesh were melting off her face.

A frigid gust ushered Maddie into the foyer as large snowflakes peppered the air. She couldn't feel the cold. Couldn't feel anything while trapped in her bodily prison. She rounded the corner and saw Lena standing on the brink of the living room. Blood dripped from a cut on her arm, and a horrified look was etched onto her features.

"Did you kill Mom?"

"He killed her. It wasn't me. He's in here with me." Maddie's admission was monotone and didn't relay any of the grief she fought to display.

"What do you mean?"

"Keeper. He's controlling me. He needs your souls. Run, Lena, because he's going to murder you next." Maddie's lips pulled apart in a goofy grin. The blood around her mouth made the movement tight.

Lena didn't move.

"Lena. Run. He's going to make me kill you." Maddie's sinister smile stretched further, and the Keeper cocked her head. "Run. Please run away from me."

In the distance, the hum of sirens sang. Lena turned toward the sound, and Maddie saw the relief bloom in her eyes.

She'll be dead before they arrive.

"Lena, get out of here."

Her sister took a step closer. "I'm not leaving you. I can get him out."

Maddie repeated the truth the Keeper whispered, "Then you'll die."

Without warning, the Keeper lunged, hands extended into claws.

"Maddie, stop!" Lena dodged the assault and slipped past her. She skirted the banister and raced up the first few stairs.

"I can't stop. He won't let me." Her honey-coated voice came out like a song, but then Maddie felt the Keeper pull back and relinquish his hold. He allowed her free rein over her voice again.

I want to hear you scream. It'll be a thrill to hear you root for her until I make you slice her throat.

"Lena!" Maddie's shrill yelp made her sister flinch. "He's coming! Run! Run! Run!"

The Keeper spun and twisted toward the steps. Maddie clawed after her sister, gaining on her.

"Lena, I'm sorry!" Maddie sobbed as a growl ripped from her chest. "Kill me, Lena. Kill me and stop him!"

Lena paused and drew back her leg, then let it fly and smashed her sole into Maddie's teeth. Her neck cracked, but the Keeper only laughed. He drew strength from her mother's soul, and the dislocated vertebrae righted themselves.

She'll have to do better than that.

He rotated Maddie's neck back into the proper position and climbed even faster.

"No! Leave her alone!"

Maddie's cries filled the house and drowned out the approaching police. If Lena could fight him off for a few more minutes, the police could save her and hopefully subdue the demon raging inside Maddie.

Lena reached the landing and ducked into their room. Maddie prayed there was an old golf club or bedpost her sister could defend herself with. Suddenly, an idea came to her.

"Get the mirror!"

The Keeper hissed and bit her tongue between her teeth.

Enough of that, little one.

Before Maddie could question the shadow's intentions, he increased the pressure on her tongue until her incisors and molars pierced the slippery muscle. For the first time, she was thankful she couldn't feel anything. The Keeper worked her jaw and gnashed her teeth. Blood welled and slid down her throat until he spat the severed tip of her tongue onto the floor. He smiled, and blood trickled over her lips.

Try to save her now.

A choked cry gargled in her throat as the stump of her tongue strained uselessly. Maddie yelled her sister's name, but the word sounded like the unintelligible bleat of a goat.

Louder. I don't think she heard you.

The Keeper flung open the door to their room and peered into the darkness, waiting for Lena to give away her position. He stepped inside. Rather than hiding under the bed as would have been Maddie's instinct, the door flew back as Lena popped out from behind. It collided with Maddie's face, and her nose crunched as the cartilage buckled under the impact. Fresh blood gushed and coated her neck and shirt in a scarlet torrent. Lena ran forth and drilled her body into Maddie's shoulder as her feral cry filled the hallway. The Keeper's eyes flared wide with genuine surprise.

Maddie's small frame absorbed Lena's hit and fell backward— too close to the stairs. The Keeper reached out to stop their fall, but Maddie's fingers were too bloody to find traction on the smooth surface of the wall. She tipped back and flipped. Maddie's legs pinwheeled over her head, and her back slammed against the hard edge of the treads. End over end, she tumbled. Her only thought was that she hoped her neck would break in the process. Her momentum finally stalled, and she collapsed in a tangled heap at the foot of the stairs. She released a pitiful sob. She was still alive.

The Keeper stretched her limbs and tested for any breaks. Her elbow jostled the broken bat at her side, and her touch sent it rolling into her periphery. If only she'd landed on its jagged spikes.

Lena raced down and paused two stairs away from her crumpled form. "Mads? Maddie, are you in there?"

Maddie wished she could answer. Wished she could tell her to forget about her and flee, but her missing tongue only allowed for guttural groans.

"Maddie, please answer me."

The Keeper twisted her body and propelled her off the floor. Lena shrieked and flashed the silver compact she had hidden in her palm. The twin discs reflected Maddie's horrifying reflection. The Keeper spun away from the mirrors. Inside, Maddie felt him writhe. She tried to tell her sister to keep aiming the compact at her, but her zombie-like moans relayed little.

The Keeper danced out of the mirror's reach. The halved bat rolled under Maddie's feet and created a hollow ringing as it shifted atop the hardwood.

Lena settled into a defensive stance. "Leave my sister, you devil. I banish you from her body."

The Keeper recoiled, anxious to escape his reflection. Maddie's heart raced upon detecting the shadow man's first real distress since he'd claimed her. Maybe they could beat him. Maybe the mirror could draw him out.

The bat kissed her foot. The Keeper hissed again and doubled over. Inside, Maddie celebrated. If anyone could stop a demonic timekeeper, it would be her sister. He fumbled with her small fingers for purchase on the bat until her fist closed around the handle, and her legs quaked as the Keeper fought to remain standing.

"Leave her alone. Go back to whatever hell you came from." Lena's command was strong and unwavering as she wielded the mirrors.

Maddie couldn't predict what would happen next as the Keeper's strength waned. Would the shadow man seep out of her? Vomit from her mouth? Or simply evaporate without enough strength to smother her soul?

The Keeper straightened, then hunched Maddie's shoulders. Blood from her broken nose and ravaged tongue painted the floor.

"Leave, Keeper!" Lena screamed.

Maddie's back snapped upward, and the bat dangled from her fingers.

"Give me back my sister!"

The Keeper grinned directly at Lena. Slowly, he shook Maddie's head. Lena jumped down the last two steps— to run or fight, Maddie wasn't sure— but the Keeper was faster.

Swinging the bat skyward, he angled the splinters up and thrust it forward just as Lena's momentum carried her down. Her eyes bulged with shock. She was unable to stop her trajectory mid-leap. Wooden teeth sliced into the bottom of Lena's jaw and exploded through her lower palate. Maddie wailed as she held the bat in place, impaling her sister and forcing her head toward the ceiling. Bubbles of blood popped over Lena's teeth. Her sister fought to pull her jaw free, but the splinters were lodged too deep and scratched the roof of her mouth pinning her shredded tongue in place.

Maddie howled as the Keeper dragged the bat free and pushed her sister to the floor. Lena landed on her back, wheezing as she choked on the river of blood that sloshed into the back of her throat. The Keeper adjusted his grip on the bat, then tossed it into the air. He caught it, shards pointing down, and drove it into Lena's neck, stabbing and twisting and scraping away her flesh.

Maddie's sobs were deep and broken. Just like with her mom, the Keeper forced her to look, to watch as he ripped the tissue and muscle apart and her sister's eyes glazed. She'd killed her whole family, unable to resist the demon possessing her body. She should have been smarter, faster. Should have listened to Sam instead of trying to stop the curse. Now, their blood was on her hands, and the Keeper had replenished his time.

A warm wave of energy flowed through Maddie as the Keeper absorbed Lena's soul—another token for his endless collection. The blood stopped running from her shattered nose and the fatigue in her muscles diminished. The Keeper dropped the bat and sighed. A feeling of contentment enveloped Maddie as he stood victorious, his mission complete. Not only had he consumed two more souls, but he'd successfully obtained a new host— one he could suckle energy from for years.

Sirens blared, and squad cars filed into the driveway. The Keeper turned to watch the cavalry pour in. Red and blue lights brightened the white landscape and illuminated Maddie's silhouette in flashing streaks. She stood in the foyer, sandwiched between her mother's caved-in skull and her sister's eviscerated throat. An army of police officers swarmed the front door, guns raised.

Maddie looked on in horror as the Keeper raised her bloodstained palms and smiled.

EPILOGUE

"What do you have?" Detective Mendez asked one of the initial officers on scene an hour later.

"Juvenile. Rhodes, Madison. Age nine. Slaughtered her mother and sister."

Detective Mendez winced. "Nine? What was the weapon?"

"Broken baseball bat and a brick from the patio."

"Christ. Has she said anything?"

The officer pressed his fingers into his eyes and rubbed his face, clearly disturbed. "Nope. She bit off her own tongue. EMTs sedated her."

The detective stared at the house and the gruesome scene just inside the door. "I had a similar case about nine, ten years ago at this same address. Guy murdered his wife and two kids. Claimed some demonic entity made him do it." He withdrew his grandfather's pocket watch and noted the time. 6:48 p.m.

He was glad he'd already had dinner because this scene would have made it impossible to keep anything down. The watch ticked, steady and true, as he placed it back in his pocket. He glanced up and flinched. In the back of the ambulance, the little girl sat strapped to a gurney, but her eyes were wide open, unblinking as she stared at him.

"Geez, that's freaky. I thought you said she was sedated?"

The officer looked over his shoulder and shivered. "Not anymore."

"Whoa. I can't imagine what would compel someone so young to flip like that. I'll follow her to the hospital. Now that she's awake, I can ask her a few questions."

The officer nodded and looked away. Detective Mendez clapped him on the shoulder and moved toward the ambulance. The little girl smiled, and her blood-caked mouth flaked slightly with the action. He suppressed a bolt of fear that tickled the back of his neck and glanced at his watch again—anywhere but the child's haunting expression.

Her hands were cuffed to the gurney, but she pointed a crimson finger at the watch.

"Do you like it?" Mendez asked. "It was my grandpa's."

The child nodded, and her grin widened. The blackening stump of her tongue was visible through the gaps in her missing teeth.

Detective Mendez cleared his throat. "Can you tell me what happened tonight? I mean, as best you can . . ."

For a brief moment, the young girl's cheerful smile faltered, and he glimpsed true heartache in her eyes. He unclipped the watch from the silver chain and handed it to the girl.

"I'll let you hang on to that while we talk, okay? Can you answer my questions with a shake or a nod?"

The child nodded slowly and stared at the watch, appearing hypnotized by the narrow hand counting time. Another chill gripped the detective, but he dismissed it. He was standing outside while a blizzard raged, after all. An EMT appeared at his side and drew his attention away from the child.

"Detective, you're welcome to ride with us."

"Thanks, that'd be great. My partner can stay and canvass the scene."

A flicker of shifting shadows spawned in the corner of his eye beneath the blue-white fluorescent light, followed by a loud clatter. The detective looked back and saw his watch down on the metal floor. He scooped it up to inspect it for damage. Luckily, the glass face was clear of scratches.

Detective Mendez frowned. The child now sat hunched over as much as she possibly could. Heavy sobs fell from her empty mouth, raw and pain-filled. Gone was the strange light in her eyes. Gone was the frozen smile. She behaved as if she were a different person.

His watch ticked loudly. A new hour had begun. The detective had a peculiar feeling, as if he'd missed something. He watched the shifting hand, entranced. The pocket watch sat warm and steady in his palm and pulsed with an energy he hadn't felt before, ticking like a beating heart.

The End

ACKNOWLEDGEMENTS

Ever since I was little, I've been drawn to darker tales. Between the Grimm Brothers and Beatrix Potter, death and macabre have always fascinated me, especially when paired alongside children. For years, I was told not to waste my time writing my own dark fairy tale collection because of market saturation. Every story I wrote had no doubt been done before, and I couldn't offer readers a "new" experience regarding the classic tales or rhymes. Yet, the desire to write my own persisted and has manifested in the anthology you now hold in your hands, and I couldn't be more thrilled.

A huge thank you to my editor, Chelsea Cambeis, for sewing up all the cracks in this collection and transforming it into the beautiful little monster it is. To my proofreader, Samantha Moran, thank you for always being there for me and taking on this project at a moment's notice. I would be lost without your sharp eye. To my cover designer, Neil J Hart, once again, I'm in awe of your ability to transcribe the jumbled images in my head into a stunning, and nostalgic cover.

To my beta readers, Amanda, J.A., and Destiny, thank you for all the time you gave to read these tales. Your feedback pushed me to make this collection even stronger. Thank you to Dakota Breann for coming up with the title for this anthology. I was wedged between so many different ideas, but your suggestion conveyed the perfect feeling.

To my brother, Zac, thank you for sharing my love of twisted, grisly stories and never shying away from my endless recommendations. To my husband, Daniel, and our wonderful kiddos, Jack and Joanna, thank you for your endless patience and support. I can't wait to read your own stories one day.

ABOUT THE AUTHOR

Caytlyn Brooke is an award-winning author known for writing books where no one is safe. She attended UAlbany, where she majored in psychology and cut two or three French classes to hang out with a cute boy. They are now married with two children and a fat orange cat. Autumn is by far her favorite season and you can find her either reading a spooky book or waiting in line for a hayride.

www.ingramcontent.com/pod-product-compliance
Lightning Source LLC
Chambersburg PA
CBHW030610310726

48979CB00003B/642
* 9 7 9 8 9 8 7 7 4 0 2 4 8 *